50 Shades of
Getting Laid

BOOK THREE

50 Shades of *Getting Laid*

BOOK THREE

Frank Holtzer

ABSOLUTELY AMAZING eBOOKS

ABSOLUTELY AMAZING eBOOKS

Published by Whiz Bang LLC, 926 Truman Avenue, Key West, Florida 33040, USA

For information contact:
Publisher@AbsolutelyAmazingEbooks.com

ISBN-13: 978-1945772115 (Absolutely Amazing Ebooks)
ISBN-10: 1945772115

To the memory of Anaïs Nin,
a dirty birdie of the first order.

50 Shades of *Getting Laid*

BOOK THREE

CONTENTS

Introduction

Here's the third entry in this spicy book series -- the stories just keep on cumming.

Needless to say, I enjoy collecting these erotic adventures and putting them to paper ... uh, computer screen. We may live in a technological age, but sex hasn't changed. It's the same old in-and-out that it's been since the caveman. Only now you don't have to hit a woman over the head with a club to fuck her. Gals have discovered their sexuality too. As you will see with some of the entries (no pun intended) in this latest collection of *50 Shades of Getting Laid*.

You'll encounter sexy volleyball players, models (professional and amateur), strippers, porn stars, and female wrestlers -- all getting fucked.

Explicit? You bet.

Hey, isn't that why you bought this book?

- Frank Holtzer
New York City

1
Volleyball In the Hamptons

At BookHampton, Roxanne came across the July issue of *Modern Bride*. A "wish book," her mother called it. And on an upper shelf she spotted a copy of *Figure Photography Annual*. She bought both publications and retired to the East Hampton beach to pour over them at her leisure.

The sun was high overhead in a cloudless sky, the temperature around 90° as she spread out her beach towel and settled down with her magazines. She'd worn a tiny bikini that she'd bought by mail order from Frederick's of Hollywood. Expensive, but the minuscule thong affair was well worth the price. Guys turned their head to stare when she peeled off her JavaWrap and stretched out like the teenage temptress in that movie *Lolita*. She'd even purchased heart-shaped sunglasses to complete the Sue Lyon image.

Of course, Roxanne was a tad more voluptuous than the petite blonde actress: Breasts swelling out of her bikini cups like overblown balloons. A few wisps of pubic hair slipping past the elastic on her bottoms. Legs like stilts.

A vision worthy of a locker-room calendar.

"Excuse me, miss," said a voice.

Looking up she saw a guy who appeared to be college material. The clue being a T-shirt that proclaimed UNIVERSITY OF OHIO. His expression was as earnest as a Jehovah's Witness. He kept cutting his eyes nervously toward some grinning guys over near a volleyball net. His classmates, no doubt.

"Yes?"

"Well, uh, my buddies and I were wondering if you'd like to play volleyball with us. We're one short."

Roxanne studiously avoided sports whenever possible. Such activity only made you sweat and ruined perfectly good hairdos. But rather than be rude she said, "Maybe one game. Then I have reading to do."

"Great," he said. "What school do you attend?"

She realized he thought she was old enough to be in college, not guessing that she was a 16-year-old private school dropout. If you could call being unceremoniously expelled "dropping out." So she lied and said, "I'll be a sophomore at NYU this Fall. I hang out in the Hamptons every summer."

"Cool. Bet you know all the good bars around here," he said.

"Absolutely." As if she was old enough to go in a bar.

"Come meet my buddies." He led her over to the gang of weekend athletes who quickly divided up into teams, each trying to claim her for its side. Finally a decision-making round of *rock-paper-scissors* put her on the Blue team. The other team was designated as Red and wore crimson headbands to prove it. This was long before states and political positions were designated as red and blue.

"You play net," instructed the captain of the Blue team. Probably so he could look at her ass throughout the game. But she didn't mind these guys getting a good eyeful. Wasn't that why she'd bought the risqué bikini?

The other side served first, an easy lob that came straight to Roxanne. "Spike it!" her team captain yelled. She made a mighty leap into the air, stretching to hit the ball and – *whoops!* – her boobs popped out of the undersized bikini top.

She won the point because nobody on the opposing side bothered to return the ball, choosing instead to stare at her ample bazongas. The pinkish nips staring back at them defiantly – at least that's the way they'd later tell it around the dorms.

"Oh my," said Roxanne, not bothering to cover herself. "Did I score a point?"

Yes, she knew how to play this game, the same principles applying as when she'd played touch football with the boys in the eighth grade. Winning was all – and what did it matter if she used a little sex to accomplish that goal?

"Your turn to serve," somebody said. Ignoring the official rules.

"This silly top seems to get in the way," she declared. "I think I'm going to take it off."

She unsnapped the catch to lots of encouraging remarks about getting "comfortable" and having "freedom of movement." Yeah, sure.

Her serve barely got the ball across the net, but she won the point anyway. All the guys were way too intent on studying the upward motion of her breasts as she gave the rubber surface of the ball an underhanded *whack!*

Even with the boys' cockamamie scoring, the game was over much too quickly for their liking. And no amount of exhortation could convince her to go for a second round. She'd won the game for the Blue team and was determined to quit while ahead.

Returning to her towel, she picked up *Modern Bride* and started to read. But she quickly grew bored with articles about place settings and gift registries, so she swapped the matrimonial magazine for the photography annual. Inside its pages were superb photographs by such masters as Irving Penn, Richard Avedon, and Helmut Newton. Many of them nudes, beautiful women stretched out in all their naked glory. *Wow!*

A shadow fell across the page. She looked up to see Mr. Earnest looming over her like a Jehovah's Witness returning with yet another attempt to pawn off a *Watchtower*. "Sorry to bother you again," he said with enough sincerity to make her believe him if he hadn't been staring at her boobs. She hadn't bothered to put her top back on. This wasn't a topless beach, but European vacationers ofttimes went for a generous application of the sun's tanning rays. So no one seemed to notice her overexposure save these horny college boys.

"No more volleyball," she cut him off before he could ask. But perhaps she'd been too quick, for his expression said that he'd had another question in mind.

"Actually, we were wondering if you'd pose for a picture with us. A snapshot to commemorate the best round of volleyball the Blue team's ever played."

She laid her magazine aside, sat up. "Sure, why not?" Reaching for her top.

"Uh, you don't have to put that on if you don't wanna."

Who didn't want her to put the top on? she smiled to herself. Thinking that she may as well give them a thrill, something to show their pals back on campus. They didn't know her name, would never see her again. What was the harm?

The blonde girl sauntered over to the volleyball net where both teams crowded around her so tightly that sweaty white skin touched her on all sides. Somebody even copped a feel of her round little ass. Mr. Earnest was designated to be the photographer, obviously the gofer of the group. More a mascot than a member. But his willingness to do their bidding obviously scored him a minor place within their ranks.

"Everybody smile at the camera," he instructed, producing a small Olympus pocket camera with built-in flash. Not that extra lighting was needed on a bright sunny day like this, other than a wink of fill-in.

Roxanne took a deep breath to emphasize her boobs, pasted on a smile, and said, "Che-e-ese!"

Fl-s-s-k!

The boys seemed pleased with the souvenir, grinning and laughing, muttering, "Who woulda thought!" and "This is one for the books!" Guess gym class didn't offer many opportunities to play volleyball with half-naked girls.

Hmm, why not throw them a bonus that would make this vacation the talk of the dorms for semesters to come?

She glanced over at her towel, where *Figure Photography Annual* lay open to a photo by Helmut Newton. The kinky German had photographed a nude woman standing there, staring defiantly at the camera, pubes brazenly showing, one from his "Big Nudes" series. The only thing that would have made the image more erotic was if the model had been surrounded by a gaggle of leering college students.

"Say, guys, would you like a picture of me completely naked?"

Their reaction did not require a vote-count. The overwhelming enthusiasm of their cheers attracted the attention of other sunbathers on this stretch of beach near Lily Pond Row. Even a lifeguard wandered over to watch as she shimmied out of her bikini bottoms and presented herself for an informal portrait.

Mr. Earnest was again ordered to take the photo, but Roxanne said, "No, ask the lifeguard to do it. Your teammate can be in this one too."

Fl-s-s-k!

The photograph captured Roxanne looking like a bare-ass cheerleader surrounded by a jubilant football team. The grins and smiles making it appear they'd just won The Big Game.

"Gee, thanks," gushed Mr. Earnest, his excitement busting through that ever-pervasive façade of sincerity. "I hardly ever get to do any of the fun stuff. I'm low man on the totem pole around here."

At that moment Roxanne had a very wicked idea: "Say, why don't we make one more snapshot? Just me and you."

"Really?"

"Uh-huh. One that will improve your status with these guys considerably."

"What do you want me to do?" Roxanne sat down on the warm sand and spread her legs, revealing the furrow that parted her wiry pubic hair. "Put your finger in me," she said.

"You mean – ?"

"Uh-huh. Finger me."

"I'd be honored."

Roxanne smiled at the camera. "Photograph this," she said to the lifeguard.

Fl-s-s-k!

"*Ooo.* Keep doing that."

Posing for these pictures had been lots of fun. Watching those slack-jawed expressions as she allowed their friend to masturbate her in front of the camera.

Fl-s-s-k! Fl-s-s-k! Fl-s-s-k! – the lifeguard kept shooting.

Roxanne's only complaint was getting sand in her twat. But it was worth the temporary discomfort. She even got off!

2
Going for A Ride

"**H**ey Judy, hold up there!"

Judith O'Connor looked around to see who was calling. Nobody she recognized. Just three guys standing next to the 9-foot statue of James Oglethorpe in Chippewa Square. A cocky effigy of an English dandy with sword in hand, it was a bronze tribute to the founder of the city of Savannah, Georgia.

"Are you boys talking to me?" she asked. They looked like locals, but she didn't recognize any of them. Maybe she *had* been away too long.

"Don't be so standoffish, girl. You know me – Stevie Davenport."

"Mikey's brother?"

"That's right. You met me years ago when I worked at the Marriott Riverfront."

Oh God, she'd sucked his dick when he delivered champagne to her room. At the time she'd been shacking up with his brother and had made a threesome of it. She'd almost forgotten about that sordid incident. "Stevie, I didn't recognize you. That was nearly two decades ago."

"That's true. Now I'm owner of Zip-Along Limo Company. These are my two drivers." He nodded at his companions, both of them grinning at her like they shared

11

some insider joke. And maybe they did.

"Congratulations."

"Thanks. I'm doin' well with my business."

"I was sorry to hear about Mikey."

"A nasty boating accident. Motherfucker was drunk at the time. Served 'im right."

So much for sibling sympathy.

"It's nice to see you, but I've got to run. I'm meeting some friends at Mrs. Wilkes." She was referring to a historic restaurant that specializes in homestyle dining, no menu, the daily selections served around the table family style. She hadn't eaten there in ages.

"You don't have to hurry. Doors don't open 'til eleven. It's barely ten o'clock."

"It's a bit of a walk from here."

"Don't worry 'bout that. We'll take you there."

"Thanks, but I don't mind the morning stroll."

"No charge for the ride. It's on me. An' it'll give us a chance to catch up on ol' times."

What *old times*? The only contact she'd ever had with Stevie Davenport was a quick blowjob in Room 323 of the Marriott Riverfront overlooking the Savannah Harbor.

"Maybe some other time."

"Don't be that way. We can take the stretch limousine."

That piqued her curiosity. "You drive a stretch on these narrow cobblestone streets?"

"Folks like it for weddings an' parties."

"I've already had a wedding." She held up her ring finger to make the point that she was married. "But I'll keep that in mind in case I throw a party"

Her marital status didn't seem to put him off. Stevie

sidled closer to whisper in her ear. "What say we throw our own party? Limo's on me."

"What kind of party – ?"

"Jus' the four of us. You, me an' the boys here. We got champagne in the limo bar. Enough to get a good buzz on. Whatcha say, sweet lips?"

What was going on here? Did he think she was a casual pickup? Guess sucking a guy's dick gave him funny ideas about you. "Sorry, but I don't think my husband would approve."

"Didn't invite him."

"Stevie Davenport, what makes you think I'd go partying with the likes of you?"

"C'mon, Judy. Don't try to play innocent with us. We seen a mighty interesting picture of you a few months ago. A real dick-raiser."

"I'll say."

"You got that right."

So that was it. That picture of her in *Playboy*. She'd been one of the girls featured in a spread on New York ballerinas. Yes, she'd been topless. Her boobs were her best feature, she'd been told. Surprisingly large for a dancer. Hmm, wonder how many other local guys had seen the picture?

"Got it right here." Stevie waved a copy of the magazine. The February issue.

"You want me to autograph it?" She extended her hand. Pissed that this revealing picture of her was being passed around by the likes of Stevie Davenport and his limo drivers.

"Sure, here's a pen."

She scribbled her name next to the image of her standing barebreasted at the practice barre.

"Now let us give you a ride around town."

"Just a ride?"

"On my joy stick."

"No, I think not. I'd rather tell my husband to kick your ass. He's a running back with the New York Giants, you know."

"Hey, no need to get testy. I was only funning you. Let's go for a ride and we'll drop you off at Mrs. Wilkes Dining Room by eleven."

Well, why not? she told herself. You couldn't blame him for trying to put the moves on her. Wasn't this sort of thing to be expected after posing for *Playboy*? Hadn't she secretly wanted guys to lust after her? Sure – just not Stevie Davenport.

"Okay, a ride," she acquiesced.

"Oh, I promise you're gonna enjoy this ride."

What the heck -- perhaps a little tickle-and-grab might be fun. It wasn't like she hadn't already sucked Stevie's dick years ago. "Let's check out how your limousine rides on these bumpy cobblestone streets," she said.

~ ~ ~

Stevie and the skinny guy were sitting with her in the backseat, the third fellow behind the wheel. Judy sank into the soft leather upholstery, sipping at a Dixie cup filled with Moët Brut.

"Where are we going?" she asked lazily, glancing out the window. Oak trees draped in Spanish moss floated by. Lots of greenery. Savannah was a beautiful town. No wonder General Sherman spared it in his infamous March to the Sea.

Stevie poured more champagne into her cup. "Jus' cruising the Historic District. Passed Forsythe Park a minute ago. We'll have you to Mrs. Wilkes on time"

"Then isn't it about time you made your move?"

"My move – ?"

"You said we were going to party. I assume you had more in mind than getting me tight on bubbly." She emptied her cup and held it out for a refill.

Stevie was so quick to pour that he sloshed champagne over them both. "Aw, damn," he muttered at his awkwardness.

"*Ooo*, I'd better take this off. It's all wet."

"Huh?" said the skinny black guy named Dayleon – Leon for short. "You gonna take yo' clothes off?"

"Here, hold my drink." She passed the cup to the skinny guy, began unbuttoning her sleek Dana Foley blouse.

"Lemme help," volunteered Stevie, all butterfingers. Feeling her boobs more than finding the pearl buttons.

"Can I help too?" said Leon, using his free hand to tug at the silky fabric.

"Boys – one at a time."

"Me first," said Stevie, smothering her neck with slobbery kisses.

"*Ooo*," Judy repeated. Accepting his awkward attentions. By now the blouse was off and Stevie was struggling with the clasp of her Victoria's Secret bra.

She got impatient with his clumsiness and reached back to help release the metal catch. *Snap!* The bra fell away, releasing her breasts like twin thoroughbreds out of the gate.

"Holy shit!"

"Damn, look-a that!"

"Ra christ." The driver – another black guy named Cedric – nearly ran off the road, his eyes following the action in the rearview mirror. "Hey, no fair leaving me out."

"Pull into one of them side streets down at the Confederate Cemetery," Stevie said between big sloppy kisses. "Then climb into the back with us, Cedric. More's the merrier."

Cedric veered into a blind alley, then hopped out to retrieve an orange cone from the limo's trunk in order to block off the alley's entrance. Wedged next to the cemetery, there were no houses on this stubby little side street, giving them a modicum of privacy.

Judy didn't object so within the next ten minutes she found herself stripped naked in the backseat of the limo with three guys pawing at her like a rerun of *Attack of the Crab Monsters.*

"Whoa!" she said when Stevie's finger breached her labia. "That's going a bit too far."

"Hey, you gonna get fucked by all t'ree of us. Why argue 'bout a finger?"

"Yeah," agreed Leon. "We gonna run a loop on you, girl."

"No way," Judy said, removing Stevie's errant hand. "We're just making out a little. Nothing more than that."

"You don't have t' play shy, Judy. These fellows know

you sucked my dick way back when. They want a hood wash for themselves."

She wiggled free, taking a jump seat across from the octopus trio. "Hold on, Stevie. That was a long time ago. Before I was married."

"C'mon, Judy. We know you a out-and-out headhunter. Why else'd you be advertising yo' wares in *Playboy*?"

"That was only a modeling gig," she tried to explain, but the words sounded hollow even to her ears.

"Oh yeah? Then how 'bout showing us a sexy-as-hell pose? Y' know, like we'd find in the centerfold."

"Something like this?" she said, parting her legs to let them view the hidden recesses. A kinky tuft of hair marking the site of her Brazilian wax.

"Hey, that's crevo."

"Fuckin' A."

"I'm gonna stick my johnson in that fine nappy dugout," Leon said, unzipping his pants. "Give you a long dicken that'll make you beg for more."

"Uh-uh," said Judy, legs snapping shut like a mousetrap. "No chance of that."

"Aw, c'mon," pleaded the livery driver. "My balls are aching for you."

"Yeah, mine too," added Cedric. A follower in the group.

Stevie said, "Be reasonable. You can't show us your pussy an' not expect something to happen."

"Well," she conceded, "I might be willing to give you boys a b.j. – if you say pretty please."

There was a cacophony of *pleases* and *pretty pleases* as the trio raced to drop trou. All were stiff as candy canes when she started licking, moving from one to the other with the timing of a plate spinner on the old *Ed Sullivan Show*.

"*Mmm-m-m*," she murmured as she wrapped her lips tightly around each shaft in turn, deep-throating them.

Stevie was the first to cum. "Damn-n-n-n," he cried with surprise. Her skilled lick-and-suck technique overcoming his hold-it-in willpower.

"Oh shi-i-t," squealed Leon as she finished him off next.

Last came Cedric with an explosive ejaculation that lathered her face with his spoot. "Girl, you one helluva nut-butter. Best skull-fuck I ever had."

"Thank you ... I think," she said, demurely wiping her chin with a tissue from her purse.

"Hey, you got a gooey fro," Stevie pointed to the globs of ejaculate in her hair. "Better clean up 'fore you go to that lunch."

"Oh my, it's almost eleven," she glanced at her Piaget. "Better drop me off at Mrs. Wilkes. But I don't think I'm going to be very hungry after that tasty appetizer."

3
Twist
And
Shout

Jason Ó Faoláin wasn't much of a dancer, but he decided the annual Mayor's Ball would be a good forum to introduce his new wife to Beauford Village. It was a black tie affair, a big deal in this small Massachusetts community outside of Boston. The idea that there might be bigots in Bo'Vil (as locals called it) never occurred to him. Contrary to his upbringing, he didn't think in terms of xenophobia and cultural intolerance. All the attention they were getting didn't surprise him – why wouldn't everybody be staring at a beautiful girl like Aki?

Several of Jason's old friends had gathered on the sidelines to discuss the hot chick he'd brought back from Japan.

"Good God Almighty!" exclaimed Moonie Moynihan. "Jason's married himself a Gook."

"No, I heard she's Japanese," said Paul Revere. Although a direct decendant of the Revolutionary War patriot, the guy was dumb as a post.

"You mean a Chink?"

"Chinks are from China," corrected Pudgy Moran, who was a walking encyclopedia. He worked for a software company in Concord. "She's a Nip, not a Chink or a Gook."

"Oh.

The three men – Moonie, Paul, and Pudgy – watched the couple in question swirl around the dance floor, oblivious to being the center of attention.

"Nice ass," Moonie observed. He was always the first to notice women's butts.

"Japanese gals usually have flat asses," stated Pudgie, a font of knowledge.

"Nice tits too," added Paul.

"Japanese girls usually have little tits," added Pudgie. "She must be a Cheese Nip."

"What's that?"

"Mixed race, a Nip with a touch of White in her."

"I've got something white I'd like to put in her," said Moonie, grasping his crotch.

Other people at the dance were upset over this racial mixing too. Some guys standing near the door were buzzing among themselves, trying to decide whether to tell the mismatched pair that this dance was for White's Only. But one of them had heard rumors about Jason Ó Faoláin. "Don't think that's such a good i-dear," cautioned Johnny Dermot. "Somebody said he killed a bunch of ragheads over in Alfghanistan."

"Hell, he wasn't ever in service," said Finnian Alby. "I hear he was a military contractor. Built bridges or something."

"Ain't no bridges in the Middle East. They don't have water for rivers."

24

"Say what you will, I'm not gonna take him on," replied Johnny. "He was a tough sumbitch in high school, captain of the football team. I remember when he broke Jimmy Brennan's jawbone. Argument over an ump's call."

"No, you don't wanna mess with him," agreed Brendan Carey. Now a used car salesman, he'd played offensive tackle in high school. "But can't say I approve of his new wife. My granddaddy died at Pearl Harbor."

"Jesus and Mary, Brendan, that was nearly 75 years ago."

"We Careys have a long memory."

"We Alby's got long dicks," said Finnian. "She's hot. I'd fuck her, yellow skin or not."

"Good luck with that," said Johnny Dermot. "Ol' Jason'd cut your balls off and hang 'em on the Christmas tree."

"To hell with Jason Ó Faoláin, I'm not staying," announced Bad Billy Ennis. "Don't have to watch him dance with a flat-faced Jap." He turned to his wingman, Tommy Finnigan. "You coming, laddie?"

"You bet your ass. Let's get outta here."

The Mayor's Ball had nearly cleared out by the time the band switched from waltzs and struck up a ditty popularized by the Beatles called "Twist and Shout." The half-dozen couples left on the dance floor picked up the pace. Guys swinging and twirling their partners like an Irish River Dance set to rock music.

Jason and his wife gave an energetic performance. However, as Jason twirled her around, one of Aki's straps broke – *snap!* – causing her right breast to pop into view. A tawny mound of flesh with a pointy brown tip.

25

The crowd by the door noticed.

"Damn, lookit that tit," observed Finnian.

"Sure's a nice one.".

"Not bad for a Jap," allowed Brendan

Jason was concentrating on his feet and didn't notice his wife's wardrobe malfunction. And Aki didn't seem to care, twisting her shoulders in time to the music, dark hair slashing wildly about her face, totally ignoring this titular exposure.

"Aki!" shouted Jason, suddenly becoming aware of his wife's fashion *faux pas*. But his admonition went unheard amid the loud, raucous music. She continued dancing with unrestrained enthusiasm.

The women in the room were gasping at the impropriety of Jason's wife's exposed breast. Their husbands gaping at this unexpected strip show. And suddenly Jason's pals were no longer concerned with her racial pedigree. Hey, a tit was a tit.

"I'm gettin' a hard-on," muttered Moonie Moynihan. Squinting at the bouncing boob.

Pudgy Moran didn't reply, hypnotized by the spectacle.

"Just think, ol' Jason's gonna be fuckin' that t'night," said Moonie wistfully.

"Gee," said Paul Revere, fantasizing by that idea. "Does fuckin' a Jap feel different?"

"Course it does," said Pudgy. "Their pussies are sideways."

"That's bullshit," replied Moonie. "I had me a Filapino when I was in the service. You couldn't tell the different 'tween her and any other girlie in the dark."

About then Jason grasped his wife hand and dragged

her off the dance floor, offering her his sports jacket. She waved him off, turning to survey the room. Yes, all the men's eyes were locked onto her like laser beams.

"Like that, do you?" she smiled at them. Reaching up to break the other strap, yanking the low-cut dress down to reveal both breasts. "How's this?"

A murmur filled the Meeting Hall, a mixture of sighs and gasps and nervous *Oh*'s.

"Oh fuck, why'd you hafta do that," grumbled Jason as he guided her outside, into the parking lot.

"I thought you were proud of my body," she pouted at his reprimand.

"Yeah, but I'm not sure this is what I had in mind for your first introduction to the good folks of Beauford Village. They can be a wee bit prudish."

"Good folks!" she scoffed. "They are the people who dropped two atomic bombs on my country."

"You weren't even born then," her husband pointed out.

"My grandmother died at Hiroshema."

"Maybe so, but it wasn't these boys that did it. Maybe their granddaddies."

"Your friends may as well get used to me." She was known for her exhibitionist tendacies. Prancing around in short-shorts and skin-tight T-shirts. As unconcerned about showing off her body as a Ginza showgirl.

Bad Billy Ennis and his pal Tommy were standing near a tricked-out Dodge Ram. The logo on the door panel said Éire Motors, the Boston car dealership where the two men worked. "Look here," sneered Billy. "Jason's Jap whore is showin' her big yellow titties."

Smak!

Billy hit the ground, barely aware that Jason had cold-cocked him with a right to the temple.

"Hey – " said Tommy.

"You got something t' say?"

"Uh, no. I was jus' headin' home."

"Then get moving. And take your big-mouthed buddy with you."

"Yessir. We're good as gone."

Aki pulled up her dress to cover her breasts. "Are all the people in Massachusetts so rude?" she asked. Not so insulted by Billy Ennis's words as by the fact he hadn't been mesmerized by the sight of her exposed boobs.

"Doesn't have as much to do with being from Massachusetts as it does with being an asshole. We call 'em Massholes."

"Have we finished dancing for the night?"

"I expect so."

Aki giggled. "We could go home and do a horizontal mambo."

Jason thought that was an excellent suggestion.

~ ~ ~

"Hear the girl made quite a showing las' night." Sitting at the breakfast table Big Brian Ó Faoláin was working hard not to crack a smile.

"You might say that," relied Jason. Not giving his uncle the satisfaction of any details.

"Sorry I weren't there."

You wanna see her titties, just ask. She'll probably give you a peek."

"Girl's mighty generous."

"That she is."

~ ~ ~

Big Brian didn't have to ask. That afternoon he found her sunning on the back patio. She was naked as a jaybird, of course. Laying there on the chaise lounge, nipples pointing at the sunny blue sky, dark bush on display.

"*Ahem*," he announced his presence. But she continued to take in the sun, not making any effort to cover herself.

"Hot out," he said. Making awkward conversation.

"Yes."

"Want something t' drink? Lemonade? Cold cider? Beer?"

"No thanks." Not moving.

Big Brian couldn't help but gape. Taking in the twin mounds of her breasts, the silky hair that populated her pubis.

Aki opened her eyes, caught him looking. "Like what you see?"

"Nice beaver."

"What is a beaver?"

"Pussy."

"Oh, that."

"Hear you showed your tits t' everybody at the Mayor's Ball last night."

"Yes, I suppose did."

"Bet tongues are wagging t'day."

"Probably. You'd think they'd never seen a woman's breasts before."

"Maybe not in public. People around here are Puritans at heart."

"What is a Puritan?" She spoke passable Enlish, but was still grappling with American idioms and phrases.

"Somebody who's got a stick up his ass."

"Oh." She liked the imagery. Rolling over, she exposed her back to the sun. Or maybe she was simply blocking his salacious view. "My strap broke," she said by way of explanation for last night's to-do.

At the moment Big Brian was focusing on her upturned butt. Quite nice. He could understand what his nephew saw in this exotic Asian girl. "Mary Edna Doyle does sewing. She can fix that dress for you."

"Mary Edna?"

"That ol' crazy woman who lives down the street. The two-story shingle house with green shutters."

"Oh her. I've seen her on her porch."

"Watch out what you say t' the ol' hag. She's Gossip Central hereabouts."

"I'm sure I'm today's topic."

"Probably so." Big Brian could feel himself getting a hard-on in the presence of this naked girl. Hope she didn't notice. Might be embarrassing, her being his nephew's new wife and all.

Aki looked up, grinned. "Does it bother you seeing me without clothing?"

"Just ain't used to having a female round this place. My wife passed away more'n ten years ago."

"Look all you want. I don't mind."

"Mighty generous of you. But maybe you better save that view for Jason. He's the one fuckin' you, not me."

She smiled. "Why, old man, are you entertaining lusty thoughts about my pretty yellow butt?"

"Well, uh – " She had him there.

"I don't mind your thinking about it. Makes for sweet dreams."

"You don't mind that men dream 'bout boning you?"

"Isn't that the idea between men and women?"

"I suspect that's true."

"I don't think I've ever met a man who didn't think about fucking me. At least for a moment or two. Straight men, that is."

"Guess I qualify as straight," he said. Acknowledging the boner showing through his trousers.

"Hm, that you do, old man. And if I wasn't married to Jason I might consider doing something about it."

"You'd fuck an old Mick like me?"

"Widow Finnbar does, I hear."

"That she does. We been keepin' company ever since her husband died five or six years ago."

"A housepainting accident, I heard."

"Fell off a ladder. He was particularly clumsy for that line o' work."

She rolled onto her side, giving Big Brian a frontal view. Those magnificent boobs. The well-manicured patch of hair. "Want to see my *manko*?" she asked matter-of-factly.

"Your what?"

"My pussy. You may as well take a look and get it over with. I know what interests guys." She opened her thighs to reveal the puffy cleft, allowing him to study this place of mystery.

"Jesus and Mary, girl."

33

"Do you like it?"

"I'll say. But that ain't something you ought to be showin' men who ain't your husband."

"Jason doesn't mind. He's proud that others find me attractive."

"What about las' night?"

"He is embarrassed by public spectacles. But it would have been okay to show one guy at a time."

"You don't say?"

"Jason's not the jealous type. He knows I belong to him."

"But you'd fuck another feller?"

"Sex is sex. Love is love."

"You'd fuck me?"

"If Jason didn't mind."

"Hm, I'll have t' think on that," said Big Brian

~ ~ ~

But it wasn't Big Brian who challenged Aki's sexual code. She'd been down to the Village to buy a new party dress (one with stronger straps), when she bumped into Bad Billy Ennis and his pal Tommy Finnigan.

"Hello there, Miss Tokyo," Billy greeted her with a smirk. He and Tommy were blocking her way on the sidewalk.

"Actually, I'm from Kyoto," she said, ignoring their rudeness.

"See you been shopping at Fiona's Finery. Whatcha buy, one-a them topless swimsuits?"

Tommy giggled. Thinking his friend's repartee was quite funny. A total suck-up.

"I used to own a Rudi Gernreich topless bathing suit.

When I lived in France."

"No shit. You showed your titties on the beach?"

"Why not?"

"There's such a thing as public decency. Do all Jap women flaunt their titties like that?"

"Some do," she replied. "Those that go to school in France. There are topless beaches at St. Tropez."

"You're a pretty loose woman for these parts."

Aki smiled. "Maybe so. But I noticed you two looking at my boobs the other night at the Mayor's Ball."

"Hard not to."

"Bet you'd like to see them again sometime." Little prick-teaser that she was.

That got Billy's attention. "You mean you'd show us your titties right here an' now?"

The smile disappeared. What jerks? "Not right here on Main Street."

"Where then?" Tommy asked. Practically salivating.

"Why not let me think about it?" she said. Realizing she'd made a bad call, offering to let these hoodlums see her boobs again.

"You promised we could see 'em," said Billy Ennis. "Ain't you as good as your word?"

"Well – " What the hell? They had seen them the other night. "Okay, but not here."

They arranged to meet at Mystery House, a roadside attraction on Boston Road. This time of year it was closed due to it being off-season for tourists. Billy's father owned it, so he had a key to the gate.

~ ~ ~

Aki spotted the big Dodge Ram as she pulled into the Mystery House parking lot. Billy and Tommy had beaten her there by fifteen minutes. Billy was known for his lead foot.

"Hi guys," she said, climbing out of her red Porsche. A gift from her husband, part of the reward for moving to Massachusetts. She had wanted to stay in France, where he'd met her.

"Shit," said Tommy Whittington, handing Billy ten bucks. He'd bet his friend she wouldn't show.

"Right this way," invited Bad Billy, holding open the gate. You could see a sloping wooden structure in the distance – Mystery House, as advertised.

Billed as the Tenth Wonder of the World (it wasn't clear what the others were), Mystery House was one of those oddities where water runs uphill and marbles roll on level floors. Some folks attributed it to optical illusions, while others swore the Laws of Gravity had been suspended by strange magnetic forces located here. The brochures called it a "Gravitational Vortex" where "up is down and down is up!"

Aki followed them into the lopsided wooden structure, noting the odd angles of walls, floors, and ceiling. She knew this was crazy, going along with this Show-and-Tell. But what the heck wouldn't be the first time she'd shown her boobies to horny voyeurs.

"So you met Jason in Japan?" Billy said. Making conversation.

"No, in France. I told you I went to school there – the Sorbonne."

"What was Jason doin' in France. Word had it, he was doing construction work in the Middle East."

"Jason was on vacation," she shrugged. "His contract had run out and he was enjoying a little Rest and Relaxation before coming home to Beauford Village."

"I take it you were part of that R&R ..."

"We got married in Paris," she said. "Under the Eiffel Tower."

"Ain't many Nips in this part of the country," Billy noted. "You're quite the oddity."

"More properly, I'm called a Nipponese."

"Nips is Nips."

"Does that rudeness mean you don't want to see my breasts again?"

Billy held up his hands. As if warding off her response. "Hold on, we ain't saying that. Go ahead – take off that top an' give us a look."

"Yesh," said Tommy. "We wanna see a Nip's nips."

"Promise not to tell?"

"Right."

"Absolutely."

"Well, okay." She reached up to unbutton her teal-blue Liz Claiborne blouse. One button, two, then three. Unveiling a lacey white push-up bra. Stark contrast to the cinnamon skin.

"Oh yeah."

"More."

She shrugged the blouse off her shoulders, tossed it to the plank flooring. Letting them take in the swell of her breasts over the cup of the lacey bra. "How's that?"

"Go on. Take it off. We wanna see your titties."

"Yeah, that's what you promised."

Aki shrugged, making the surface of her boobs ripple. "As you wish."

Billy and Tommy watched as she unhooked the clasp and let the white bra fall away. Her nipples as stiff as two lumps of caramelized sugar. "Take a good look. I don't mind."

"Damn," blurted Billy. "Them's quite a pair."

"You said it," added his pal.

"Thank you, boys." She bent down to retrieve her blouse.

"Wait up. We wanna see the rest."

"The rest – ?"

"Yeah," Billy nodded. "Get completely naked. Show us everything."

"That wasn't the deal," Aki protested.

"Rules been changed," said Billy. "You're alone here with me an' Tommy. Ain't nobody to say what happens."

"Look but not touch?" she tried to establish some rules.

"Haw to that," said Billy. "Ain't no need to be so standoffish. We gonna welcome you to America in a proper manner."

"That's right," said Tommy. Grabbing his crotch to make the point. "Think of us as the Welcome Wagon."

Aki kicked off her pumps and fiddled with the catch on her pleated Ann Taylor skirt. *Snip!* – it fell away, settling at her feet. Leaving her in white bikini panties.

"There," she said. "But I'm not sure who's welcoming whom."

"Can't believe we're gonna fuck Jason's Jap wife," said Tommy. "Who would-a thought?"

"That's not goimng to happen," she said. "This is merely a private viewing, not an invitation to have sex."

"We'll see 'bout that," grinned Bad Billy, winking at his friend. Tommy grabbed her arms, pining her from behind.

"Hey – !" she squealed.

Billy pulled her panties down with one swift yank. "Who-ee, look-a that silky pussy hair. Ain't that a pretty sight?"

Tommy tried to lean around her to see, loosening his grip enough that she managed to twist free. "Massholes," she spat.

Aki tried to distance herself from the assailants, but tripped over the panties bunched around her ankles.

"Gotcha," said Billy, steadying her while copping a feel. Hands cupping her breasts, he liked their mushy texture.

"Let me go!"

"Bend over an' spread them butt cheeks. I'm gonna fuck you in the arse."

"Like hell you are – !"

"Girl, you gonna get yourself a dicking. You come out here an' pull off your clothes, whattaya expect?"

"My husband will kill you."

"Right, an' the Easter Bunny's gonna bring me some colored eggs."

Tommy sniggered at his friend's snappy repartee. "I wanna feel them big titties too," he said, pushing Billy aside.

That gave Aki a second chance at escape. Stepping out of the panties, she quickly moved out of their reach.

"Don't run away," ordered Billy, trying to catch her arm. But the tilted angle of the Mystery House floor threw him off balance, causing him to fall.

"*Umph*," he groaned as his head hit the planks.

Tommy had unzipped his trousers and pulled out his wiener, thinking he was about to get laid. He was unprepared for his buddy's tumble. Aki used his awkward stance to her advantage, kneeing him in the groin.

"*Aggggh!*" Tommy screamed, doubling over.

She made a run for her car. Putting miles between her and those two Irish-American hoodlums. Arriving home in record time.

~ ~ ~

Big Brian raised an eyebrow when she walked in completely naked. "Been sunning again?"

"No," she said, plopping down on the couch. "Billy Ennis tried to fuck me where the sun don't shine."

"You don't say? Never did like that boy. But don't worry. Jason will kick his ass for you."

"That's what I'm afraid of. So we're not going to tell him."

Big Brian seemed disappointed. "You sure? Billy Ennis an' that Finnigan boy need their asses kicked, you ask me."

"Maybe so. But we'll leave that to someone else."

"Hell, girl. I'll do it if you want me to. Them two punks ain't got no backbone."

"Let's simply forget the whole experience. I didn't actually get fucked. And those two idiots had already seen my boobs at the Mayor's Ball. No harm, no foul."

"Okay, if you say so."

"I better go get some clothes on."

"Don't bother on account of me."

She glanced in the old man's direction, noticed the bulge in his trouser. "Oh? Have you changed your mind about fucking me?"

"Well," said Big Brian with a wink, "I don't expect an old feller like me's got much of a chance at that, considering you turned down two studs like Billy and Tommy."

"Ha. I would have fucked them if they had asked nicely."

"And me?'"

"Ask nicely."

So he did.

4
Building A Modeling Portfolio

"**L**ike my new outfit?" asked Amanda Wentworth, modeling it for her boyfriend. A dark-blue Armani cocktail dress and knockoff Christian Dior sunglasses – hip and elegant at the same time!

"Bet that set your MasterCard back a pretty penny," Jack Spivek remarked as he glanced up from his book. Some thick tome on string theory. He was a grad student at UCLA.

"Yes, but don't you just love it?"

"Pretty as a picture."

"Hm, wish I had some pictures of me in this. For my portfolio."

"You still want to be a model?" Amanda had just graduated from Beverly Hills High and like many California girls aspired to be a model or actress.

She twirled to provide a 360° view of the sleek Armani dress. "Don't you think I'm pretty enough?"

He knew this to be a question loaded with dynamite. "You look like you stepped right outta the pages of *Harper's Bizarre*," he responded. Taking no chances.

"*Bazaar*," she corrected.

"Whatever." He knew more about particle physics than

47

fashion.

"Why don't you borrow my brother's camera and snap some pictures of me in this lovely outfit?"

"Your brother Brad's out of town," he reminded her. "Went to San Francisco." As a pharmaceutical salesman, Amanda's brother Bradley Wentworth was constantly on the go.

"Rats. I wanted to get some photos before I take this back to The Bountiful Boutique."

"Back?"

"You know I can't afford this, Jack. It's a genuine Armani. *Beaucoup* bucks."

"I knew that. Just wasn't sure you did."

"Doesn't someone have a camera you could borrow?"

Jack thought about it. "Maybe Paul Ferris will loan us his."

"Paul Ferris?"

"A new guy who transferred in from Cal Tech. Going for a doctorate in Physics like me. He was showin' off a new camera jus' last week. And he's been wanting to meet you."

" – me?"

"Said he heard I was dating the prettiest girl in L.A."

"I wouldn't exactly call it dating. We've been playing house for over six months now." Ever since she graduated from Beverley Hills High. Jack had repeatedly proposed, but she thought marriage might interfere with a modeling career.

"Aw, you know what I mean."

"Invite him along. He can watch you snap my pictures. I don't mind having an audience," smiled Amanda.

Little did she know the import of that suggestion.

~ ~ ~

They decided to shoot the photos in an abandoned warehouse off Little Santa Monica Boulevard. Jack didn't consider himself much of a photographer, but Paul Ferris' state-of-the-art Minolta did everything but tell the subject when to say "cheese."

Ferris was a tall sandy-haired guy from Maryland. He had a casual air about him, like a Brainiac who had just aced his grad school entrance exam. He usually wore khaki slacks and tan Polo shirt, which added to the laidback collegiate image. Today he was wearing a sharkskin black suit.

"We'll grab a few quick shots," Jack explained. "Amanda's trying to put together a modeling portfolio."

Paul Ferris nodded. "She certainly looks striking in that dress."

"No wonder with its price tag."

Amanda was standing in the center of the rubble-strewn warehouse, a vast cavern with peeling paint and tall industrial windows with broken panes. She looked as poised as a charm school grad on her first job interview. "Ready, dear?" she called to Jack.

"Yep, here goes. You pick the poses, I'll press the button."

She twisted around, looking back over her shoulder. "Try this," she said.

Fl-s-s-k! – he made an exposure.

She shifted her position, a profile. "And this," she cued him.

Fl-s-s-k!

"And this."

Fl-s-s-k! Fl-s-s-k! Fl-s-s-k! – a series of poses followed. Dynamic stances that looked terrific through the digital camera's viewfinder.

Jack was feeling pretty good about the photos he was getting here today.

"She could be a pro," Paul Ferris commented from the sidelines.

Jack nodded. "Gotta admit it's hard to take a bad picture of her."

Amanda waved to get their attention. "Hey, guys, are we through?"

"May as well get a few more shots, while we're at it," said Jack. He turned to the other man. "Hey Paul, why don't you get in the picture with her?"

"I'm no model."

"Don't matter. I'm no photographer."

The tall man chuckled as he walked over to join Amanda in a patch of sunlight. "Just tell me what to do," he said to her.

"Simply stand here and I'll strike some poses. Nothing to it."

"Okay."

Fl-s-s-k! – Jack got off a shot. Amanda next to Ferris, her arm linked with his like a couple out for a stroll.

"How was that, dear?" she asked.

"Good. Do another one."

Amanda threw her head back to simulate a laugh, hands grasping her partner's arm.

Fl-s-s-k!

"Again."

Her head on Paul's shoulder, snuggling close.

Fl-s-s-k!

"Good, good."

"Here, let me take off the jacket," she said. Tossing it aside. "To show off this rufflely blouse."

"Don't get that jacket dirty on that floor," cautioned Jack. "I don't wanna hafta buy it."

"Oh silly." She gave him a pose that emphasized her bustine. Paul eyeing her with interest.

Fl-s-s-k!

"You can do better than that," Jack jibed.

"Oh yeah?" She slipped the straps off her shoulders, allowing the dress to slide to her waist, revealing a lacy white strapless bra. "How about that?"

"Sexy," he said.

"Sexy," Ferris agreed.

Fl-s-s-k!

"Want more?"

"Up to you. It's your portfolio."

With that, she reached behind her back and unsnapped the bra. Letting it fall away. "There," she said. Unmindful that her pink nips were on display to her boyfriend's astonished chum.

Fl-s-s-k!

"Hey!" said Jack. "That was a good one."

"I'll say," echoed Ferris. Getting an eyeful.

"Hold on a sec," said Amanda as she unhooked the blue dress and let it fall to the concrete floor. She was wearing bikini panties, white lace that matched the aforementioned bra.

"Paul, put your arms 'round her waist."

"Like this?"

"Yeah, that's good."

Fl-s-s-k! – it was an erotic shot, a semi-naked woman posing with a fully dressed man.

"Another."

Amanda leaned into Paul Ferris' arms, tips of her breasts pointing toward the camera. "How's this?"

Fl-s-s-k!

"Great – but don't know if I'd put that in your portfolio."

"Oh, we're way beyond my modeling portfolio. These pictures are meant to give you a stiffie."

"Well, it's working," admitted Jack.

"Want more?"

"Uh – "

"Here's one. Paul, put your hands on my boobs," Amanda prompted.

The man looked surprised. "You sure?"

"Go ahead," she said. "It's just a picture."

Fl-s-s-k! – an image of the befuddled grad student squeezing her breasts, a wide grin crossing his face.

"*Mmm*, that's good," she purred. Putting her hands over Paul's to hold them in place. Turning her head to nuzzle on his neck as if they were lovers.

Fl-s-s-k!

"Holy shit, Jack. Is this okay with you?"

"She's a big girl. I ain't the boss-a her."

"Let's get some really good shots," she said, as if trying to prove her boyfriends words.

"Like what?" asked Jack.

"Like this," she replied. Sliding the white panties down her legs and kicking them off.

"Jesus," said Paul. Staring at her exposed pubes, a perfect of wiry black hair.

"Ready," she said, raising her arms to link them around Paul's neck. Elevating the twin mounds of her breasts, causing the nipples to point skyward.

Fl-s-s-k!

"Not bad," Jack grinned.

"I can do better," she averred. Swinging her shoulders around and pulling Paul's head down against her large bazongas. "How about that?"

"You're sure you want a picture like this?" asked Jack.

"It'll be a sexy shot. Right, Paul?"

"*Mmph*," he mumbled, face burrowed against her breasts.

"Go ahead, suck on them," she said. Smiling defiantly at the camera.

Fl-s-s-k! – Jack caught a clear image of his colleague's mouth covering the tip of her left breast. An intimate gesture that would inspire a hard-on with future viewers.

"Maybe we oughta stop here," muttered Jack, lowering the camera.

"Coward. Paul and I were just getting warmed up."

"We got some good shots."

Amanda pouted. "Don't you want at least one of us naked together?"

" – naked?" sputtered Paul Ferris.

"Dear?"

"Well," Jack hesitated, studying the sight of his naked girlfriend with another man. "Maybe just one."

"Then we'd better make it count. Right, Paul?"

"Uh, sure."

"Here," she offered, "let me help you get undressed." Her fingers nimbly unbuttoning the grad student's shirt, then going for his belt. "These next photos will be fun."

These? Jack thought. Hadn't they agreed on just one? He said, "Amanda – ?"

"Don't be a wuss, dear. Paul's game."

"Oh, what the heck," concurred Ferris as he stepped out of his trousers.

"Shorts too," she prompted.

"Yeah, okay." He doffed the white briefs.

"Ooo, what a nice dick."

"Uh, thanks," he sputtered.

Amanda struck a pose, one that offered a frontal view of both of them.

Fl-s-s-k!

"Got it," said Jack.

"How about one over by the window?" she suggested.

"You're the one picking the poses," said Jack.

Smiling, she led her partner to a windowsill, where she planted her butt and parted her legs to expose her sex.

"Jesus," Paul Ferris said as he stared at her puffy labia. The inner lips were slightly parted, offering a hint of pink.

"*Ooo*, look. You've got a boner," Amanda observed. Grasping it to guide him forward.

"Whoa!"

"Go ahead, put it in me."

"Hold on, I can't fuck you with Jack standing there."

"Why not?"

"Well, uh – " He cast a quick glance in her boyfriend's direction. Not sure what to do. This girl was beautiful, naked, and seemingly willing. Difficult to pass that up.

"She's just teasing you," Jack said, focusing the Minolta's lens on them.

"Teasing? We'll see who's teasing," she said, wrapping her legs around her partner's waist.

"Amanda – !"

"Get a photo of this!" she said defiantly. Thrusting her hips upward to implant his shaft inside her.

To everyone's surprise, Jack took the picture. *Fl-s-s-k!*

"Oops, sorry," she blurted. "Guess I got a little carried away."

"May as well keep going," her boyfriend said with a shrug.

"You're sure?"

"Damage's already done, hon. May as well get some sexy pictures."

"If you say so."

Paul didn't need any encouragement. He leaned forward to enter her again, burying his shaft in her moist depths.

"Woo. Let's give my boyfriend some really sexy fuck pictures."

"My pleasure," Paul said. Pumping away at her like a jackhammer. His tumescent organ sliding in and out with a steady *squish-squish* rhythm.

Fl-s-s-k! Fl-s-s-k! – Jack captured the coital action. His girlfriend and a near-stranger.

"Dear, you're sure about this?" she grunted. Her hips matching her partner's rhythm.

"Too late to ask that question. We may as well get a few pictures for my private album."

"Oh, I'll give you some good pictures, alright."

Amanda pressed her hands against her partner's ribs to steady him. "Pull out before you cum," she instructed.

"Birth control?"

"No, it'd make a great photo, you shooting your spunk onto my belly."

"Oh."

Fl-s-s-k! Fl-s-s-k! Fl-s-s-k!

Jack was recording the sexual union with the digital camera, seemingly oblivious to the fact that it was his girlfriend there on the window ledge fucking this near-stranger with all the fervor of a wanton whore.

"Dear, want a really good picture?" gasped Amanda. "What if I let him cum in my mouth?"

"Go for it."

Amanda waited until her partner muttered, "Okay, I'm ready."

"Pull out," she said.

"Oh, right."

"Here," she said, scooting down to the floor and aiming his cannon at her face as he shot his load.

Fl-s-s-k! – Henri Cartier-Bresson couldn't have done a better job of capturing the Decisive Moment, a stream of ejaculate forming a perfect arc into her open mouth.

"Damn, Amanda. That was hot."

"Thank you, dear."

"You got a dab of jism there on your chin."

"*Mmm*," she licked it off.

"Now whatta I do 'bout ol' Paul here?" He looked down at the naked man who had collapsed onto the floor. Spent from his exertions.

"Give him back his camera and send him home. He's

had a tiring afternoon."

"Hm, better take the chip outta it first. Don't need these pix being passed around the physics department. Bad 'nuff, he'll be bragging that he fucked my girlfriend."

~ ~ ~

As predicted, Paul Ferris did tell some of his colleagues about boffing Jack's cutie-pie girlfriend, but nobody believed him. Why would a beautiful young woman like Amanda Wentworth have sex with this jerk in front of her boyfriend? Ferris was branded as a poor liar, an assessment that would hamper his career in future years.

~ ~ ~

When Jack downloaded the photos, he went through them one by one with Amanda. Jesus, they were hot. That night, they made love like minks in heat.

"*Woo*, that was wonderful," she said as they lay there in post-coital exhaustion. "We should make lots more photos if they get you horny as that."

"This is the last time we do this. Can't be letting guys screw my girlfriend."

"But you enjoyed seeing me with Paul. I could tell."

"True. It was like you were an X-rated actress. Putting on a show for me."

"Really?"

"Yep. You're as pretty as any of those famous porn stars."

"Thank you, dear."

"But no more sex with other men."

"Back to monogamy?

"Right."

"Boring."

"Hey, that's the rule."

"Oh, okay. Want to look at the pictures again, then go a second time?"

"I'm up for it," he said. A deliberate double entendre.

5

Bending the Rules

Richard Wheeler had borrowed his brother's Boston Whaler to take the guy from the home office for a sightseeing cruise around the island. An attempt at bonding between two men who sometimes worked together on offshore investments. Your bonus could depend on a good analyst, as Richard often said.

Jessica's husband had invited her along for the ride that Sunday afternoon. "Show Brian a good time," he instructed. "I want to get in good with him."

Dutifully, Jessica packed a picnic basket of cold chicken and beer. Not being much of a cook, she could always count on KFC for a passable meal. The bottles of Red Stripe (Richard's favorite) were on ice in a Styrofoam cooler that she'd bought at Fosters Food Fair. Under her shift, she wore a tiny yellow halter-top and bright-red Carnaby Street hot pants that were so tight you could see the cleft of her sex when she sat down. Brian ought to like *that*!

They left from the Barcadere Marina on the north side of Grand Cayman, circumnavigating the island in a counter clockwise direction, rounding the eastern tip at the mariculture turtle farm, past Dog Town, and cruising along sandy Seven Mile Beach. They chugged down to George

Town, then rounded the hump and headed along the southern shore keeping parallel to East West Road. After passing the village of Bodden Town, Richard steered around the hulks of sunken ships, some of them left over from the Bay of Pigs. This stretch of blue-green water was a snorkeler's paradise.

Out past Old Isaac, they spotted a sandy beach and anchored just offshore. Looked like a good spot for a picnic, Richard allowed. Nobody was around and you couldn't see down to the beach from the nearby road. Plenty of privacy.

Brian Weatherly stripped down to his swim trunks and jumped into the waist-high water, reaching up for the picnic basket. Richard shucked his shirt and picked up the beer cooler to tote it ashore. He looked quite fit in the Johnny Weissmuller trunks that Jessica had bought him for his birthday.

"Need some help?" Richard asked his wife as he got his footing on the seafloor. Mostly sand, but you had to be careful of sea eggs, those spiny urchins that could sting like the very devil. That's why he was wearing his new Speedo water shoes, protective footwear with thick soles and an internal exoskeleton.

"No, I'm fine," she said, standing up in the boat. "I'll just dive in and swim ashore."

When she shucked off her cotton shift, he noticed she was wearing her halter-top and hot pants. "Where's your bathing suit?"

"Didn't bring one. If Brian doesn't mind, I'll just go skinny dipping."

"F-fine with me," he lisped. Carefully holding the picnic basket over his head to keep the food dry. "Promise I won't l-look any more than's necessary."

She liked his sense of humor. "Look all you want, I don't mind."

"Jessica – "

"Pish, dear. We're all friends here," she said as she untied her halter straps and exposed her perky boobs to the bright sunshine.

"S-sun's pretty bright. Be careful you don't b-burn those twin beauties," advised Brian Weatherly. "Could be painful if you and your honey get frisky tonight."

"Why wait 'til tonight to get frisky?" she teased as she tugged off the tight red shorts. She wasn't wearing panties underneath, providing an unsecured view of her thick pubes. "I'm up for sex on the beach."

"Hey, don't embarrass our guest."

"Oh, I'm sure Brian has seen people have sex before. In fact, why don't we invite him to join us?"

"You m-mean a threesome?" stammered Brian. Pronouncing the word as *twee-some*. A certain Elmer Fudd quality to his speech. He'd had a speech impairment since childhood. It became more prominent when he got excited.

"Dear," she addressed her husband, "it would be the hospitable thing to do."

"Don't think I'm up to it on an empty stomach," Richard replied, trying to make light of her suggestion. "I'm ready for some fried chicken."

"Why don't you go ahead and eat while Brian and I get started. You can join in later." Before he could respond, she dived over the side of the boat, her naked form disappearing beneath the blue-green water. Despite the water's transparency, the refraction of sunlight made it hard to follow the mermaid's path. She emerged a few feet from shore in knee-deep water, waving for them to join her on the tiny strip of sand.

The backdrop of foliage and the curve of the shore made this a haven from the prying eyes of passing boats. She pranced down the beach, unconscious of her nudity, looking for a nice spot to encamp.

"Over here," she called to her two companions. "There's shade from these cabbage palms."

Richard and Brian trudged along the surf until they were parallel to her campsite, then headed for the shaded area where she waited, hands on hips, her breasts as prominently displayed as the masthead on the bow of a ship.

"Can't wait to get at this chicken," Richard said, shifting the subject away from Jessica's proposed tryst. He knew she was just kidding, right?

But Jessica wasn't willing to let it go so easily. "Here, Brian," she reached down to grasp his waistband, "let me help you get out of those trunks."

"Okay," he shrugged. It came out *o-tay.*

Jessica pushed the wet fabric down his thighs in one quick motion, freeing a cucumber-sized penis that had been neatly circumcised. "Oh my," she said. "That's quite an attractive specimen."

Richard was frowning now. Unusual for his passive expression to reveal what he was thinking. "Jessica, this is not a good idea," he said grimly.

"You eat while I fool around with your friend Brian. Then I'll do you. Save me a drumstick, okay?"

She dipped to her knees and took Brian in her mouth, the full lips surrounding it like a gasket. "Oh, shit," he said, but it sounded like *thit*.

"Jessica!"

"*Mmm-mph,*" she replied, otherwise ignoring her husband's admonition.

Within seconds she had the man's organ standing up at a 45° angle, as stiff as a lead pipe.

Brian appeared to be as surprised by the consequences of her lip action as Richard. He looked helplessly at the top of her head, bobbing up and down like a pump, determined in its mission.

"There," she said. "Ready for action." She lay down on the sand, pulling him with her, wrapping her long legs around his hips.

"Wait, Jessica, I c-can't do this," protested Brian.

"Sure you can. Richard doesn't mind."

"But I do," he said, pulling away. "You see, I'm gay." *See* came out as *thee*.

She cut her eyes toward Richard. "You knew this all along and let me make a fool out of myself?"

Her husband shrugged. "You didn't give me much opportunity to tell you."

Brian looked sheepish. "Gotta admit you give a great blowjob, boy or girl."

"Thanks, but I feel like a fool," Jessica acknowledged her *faux pas*.

"You can f-finish me off if you want," he offered.

"Why not?" she smiled.

Richard shook his head wearily. "Go ahead. I did tell you to show Brian a good time."

Jessica returned to the task at hand. Brian Weatherly might be right, she thought, a pair of lips was a pair of lips. But the opposite was true too. A stiff dick was a stiff dick, gay or straight.

She finished her task, then wiped her lips daintily with her tongue.

6
Photographs On
A Summer Day

James Franklin fancied himself a photographer, always snapping pictures. More persistent than a Japanese tourist. He owned a Nikon with a digital back, a pricy camera that did everything but say, "Che-e-ese!"

He and his wife Alice were part of our crowd, along with Aaron and Betsy Coulter. My wife Barb liked to get together with them on weekends – picnics, movie parties, backyard cookouts, Monopoly tournaments, you name it. I guess I enjoyed these get-togethers too -- but did they have to be *every* damn weekend?

On the weekend in question we were having a Sunday afternoon picnic, a cornucopia of country ham, deviled eggs, cole slaw, and banana pudding. We'd picked an old abandoned farm up near the Blue Ridge Parkway, a patchwork of fenced-off pastures and an empty two-story frame house that slumped sadly with disrepair. The sky was a robin's egg blue with a yellow butterball sun. The weather was warm, 98° in the shade.

We'd polished off the food and washed it down with three bottles of Yellowtail Chardonnay. Guess everybody was feeling pretty good, a little buzz on.

"Hey, Betsy, smile at the birdie," said James, aiming his camera at Aaron's wife.

"Birds, what birds?" she looked up into the trees.

Fl-s-sk!

"Darn it, James, you caught me with my mouth open," Betsy complained. He was always snapping pictures when someone was off guard. Candids, he called them.

"Now one of you, Barb." He focused his camera on my wife.

"Forget it, James. Take one of Alice."

"Oh, he has dozens of albums filled with photos of me," his wife rolled her eyes. "Candids, vacation snapshots, portraits, pinups, you name it."

"Pinups?" Aaron picked up on the theme. "I'd like to see some pinups of you."

"Yeah, me too," I nodded. "How about it, James?"

"That's up to Alice," grinned James.

"I don't mind," responded his wife. "Next time you're over we'll have a show-and-tell. Maybe James can shoot some pinups of Betsy and Barb too. That way I won't feel embarrassed by you guys looking at half-naked photos of me."

"Oh, you want us to be embarrassed along with you?" laughed Betsy. "I'm not gonna do it unless Barb does."

My wife shrugged. "That's up to Sam. I'm not showing off my goods unless he says it's okay."

I grinned. "Might be fun seeing pinups of you girls."

"Yeah, all our wives showing some skin, that'd be cool."

"Oh, you horny guys," laughed Barb.

James tilted his head to study the women. "What say we try a few practice shots?"

"Right now?" exclaimed Betsy. "My hair's a mess. My nails are chipped. I'm wearing hardly any makeup. No, some other time if you please."

He turned to my wife. "Barb, how 'bout you? Your bob cut just needs a shake of the head. Your nails look fine. And you're wearing lipstick and mascara."

"Oh, what the heck," she agreed. "What do you want me to do?"

James glanced around. "Hm, how 'bout standing beside that old stone fence. The light's good over there."

"Okay," she shrugged. Being a good sport.

James steadied his camera, centering Barb's form in the viewfinder. She looked darned good, her feldgrau-green jumpsuit hugging her curves. "Turn your chin more this way," he instructed.

"Like this?"

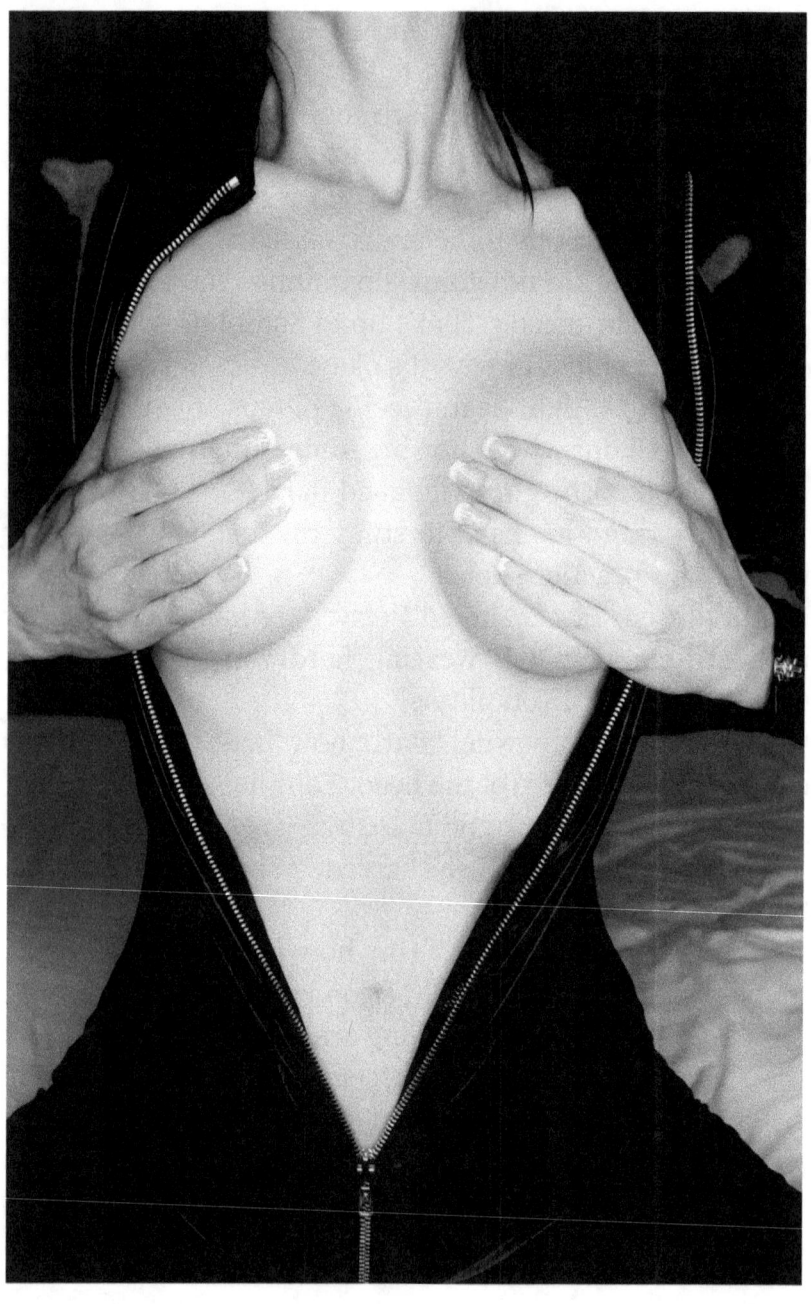

"That's perfect," he said. "Now take a deep breath and smile."

She offered a dazzling Pepsodent display.

Fl-s-sk!

"Nice," he encouraged. "For this next one, unzip your jumpsuit about halfway down."

"Uh, I'm not wearing a bra."

"All the better."

With a what-the-heck shrug, she tugged downward on the jumpsuit's zipper tab. *Zip-p-p-p!* The resulting V exposing a swath of alabaster skin. The swell of her breasts forming a)(that seemed to be trying to escape their confines.

Fl-s-sk!

"Yes, that's very sexy. Now turn more to your side. Puff out your chest."

Barb seemed to be getting into it. She swiveled her shoulders and provided a profile that emphasized her ample breasts. You could see the undercurve of one of her big boobs, its gravitational droop, the nipple barely concealed by the shiny fabric of her unzipped jumpsuit.

Fl-s-sk!

"Turn back this way," directed James. "That's it. Now how 'bout flashing one-a your tits."

"Sam?"

I shrugged. Enjoying the view.

"Well, okay." She tugged aside the shiny fabric, allowing a plump breast to pop into view. The pale flesh quivering like Jell-O. The areola wide and pink, punctuated with a stiff nip. A familiar sight to me, but an exotic revelation to my friends.

79

"Holy crap!" sighed Aaron.

"Way to go, Barb," encouraged James' wife.

My wife giggled.

Fl-s-sk!

"Both of them now," instructed James.

Barb shrugged the bodysuit off her shoulders, pulled her arms out of the sleeves. The shiny Lycra garment hanging at her waist, leaving her completely topless. The sight of her bared breasts drew a low whistle from Aaron.

"Glad you like 'em," my wife responded. Deliberately giving them a little jiggle for his benefit.

"Barb, you slut you," teased Betsy.

"I am, aren't I?" my wife agreed with a broad smile.

Fl-s-sk!

"Squeeze them between your arms," said James, focusing on the twin mounds.

"Like this?" Barb compiled, squishing her breasts together like two balloons about to pop.

Fl-s-sk!

"How 'bout getting all way naked. Try a few artistic nudes."

"Artistic? You just want some pictures of my pussy," accused my wife.

"So?" he responded. "You gonna chicken out?"

Barb turned to the other wives. "How about it, Betsy? I'm not going to do this unless you and Alice do it too."

"I don't know about that," Betsy demurred. "Completely naked?"

"No big deal," said Alice. "I'm not shy." Unbuttoning her red-checkered blouse, she tossed it aside. Then unzipped her Bermuda shorts and stepped out of them, leaving her in bra and panties. A matching set, pink lace with a heart-like design. "Well, Betsy, what are you waiting for?"

Aaron's wife tentatively lifted the hem of her camisole top, exposing bare midriff. "Are you two really getting naked?"

"Nary a stitch," James answered for them. "C'mon, it'll be a lark."

"I'm game," said Alice. To prove the point, she unhooked her bra and let it fall to the ground. Her oversized breasts tumbled out, DD cups for sure. Puckery pink nipples like dots atop great mountains.

"Holy moley," I blurted. They were humongous, much larger than they appeared in her loose-fitting clothing.

The panties were next to go, leaving James' wife completely starkers. Her pubes as bristly as steel wool. "Go ahead, Barb. You too, Betsy."

Betsy Coulter pulled the camisole over her head and shook her hair free. She wasn't wearing a bra, her apple-sized breasts standing up without support. Nipples like tiny rosebuds. "Okay, there you are," she murmured, obviously embarrassed.

"All the way," urged James. "You too, Barb."

My wife shrugged and wiggled out of her pantsuit. Her panties were thin, revealing a dark triangle. A tease.

"Rest of the way," urged James.

"Here goes," she said, sliding the skimpy undies down her long legs and stepping out of them.

"Nice pussy," complimented James.

"I knew you just wanted to see it."

Fl-s-sk!

"Now I've got a picture of it too."

"You rat."

"Now you, Betsy," he said.

Betsy Coulter blushed scarlet as she dropped her shorts and removed her white cotton panties. She shaved, her pubic mound as bare as a cut-down rain forest. "Aaron likes it hairless," she explained nonchalantly.

"I love a bald eagle," he affirmed. Proud of his wife's surprise.

Fl-s-sk! – James captured the smooth surface of her *mons veneris*.

"Great shot," he trilled. "Now let's get one of all three of you together."

The girls lined up along the rock fence, a triptych of nudity. Locking arms, they smiled at the camera lens.

Fl-s-sk!

"All of you sit on the fence and spread your legs," James ordered. "I wanna get a group pussy shot."

"Told you," my wife said. But she obediently positioned her bottom against the stone surface and offered a split beaver. Her girlfriends adopted a similar pose, showing all.

Fl-s-sk!

My wife's twat was a familiar terrain of wrinkles and folds. Betsy's was a puffy little slit. Alice's was a wide gash that offered a hint of pink interior. All different, yet all the same.

"How 'bout a shot of guys with the gals?"

"Sure," I said. Ambling over to stand beside my wife.

"No, you gotta be naked too," James insisted.

"Hey – " protested Aaron.

"Fair's fair," said his wife. "If I've gotta stand here with

82

my tits showing, you've gotta get naked too."

"Oh, all right." He started to unbutton his shirt.

"You sure you want me to show you fellows up with my long dick," I joked. Truth is, it's regular sized, but I know guys are sensitive about that."

"Ooo, I wanna see," Alice said boldly.

"Me too," squeaked Betsy.

"He's just bragging," said Betsy's husband. "I've stood next to him at urinals. My dick will give his a run for the money any ol' day."

When Aaron and I had both stripped, you could see it was a close call, both about the same length despite their growing tumescence.

"Wow, look at that," exclaimed Betsy when James got naked. His wanger was a good two or three inches longer than mine and Aaron's.

"Could-a told you," boasted Alice. "I get to experience that Roto-Rooter every single night of the week. James is a great fuck."

"Yeah, he's a fuck, all right," I muttered sourly. Bad sport that I am.

"Every night?" said Barb. Probably a dig about our sporadic sex life.

"Sometimes twice," beamed Alice Franklin. Her big bazongas swaying as she shifted her position on the fence.

"Okay, for the next photograph," James steered us back on track, "guys with gals. Remember?"

I stood next to Barb, my hand resting on her ass. "This will be a hoot," I grinned. Like a kid going skinny-dipping with the gang.

"No, no," barked James. "Not with our own wives. Mix 'em and match 'em for the picture. Sam, you with Alice. Aaron with Barb. And me with Betsy."

"Huh?" I responded, a bit dumbfounded by the suggestion.

"C'mon, I'll set my timer, get all of us in one shot. That'll be a doozy for the ol' family album."

"Works for me," said Aaron, eying my wife eagerly.

"Oh boy, me with Sam," declared Alice, sliding off the stonewall and scampering over to where I stood. Her giant-sized melons bouncing with each step. Holy cow!

Yes, pun intended.

The others took their places with assigned partners, Barb looking doubtful as she settled in next to Aaron. "Okay, link your arms around each other's waist, smile at the camera," instructed James as he balanced the camera on a tree stump and pressed the timer button.

Z-z-z-z – fl-s-sk!

"Got it. A photo of friends being very friendly."

"Oh, you can do better than that," said Alice.

"Like what do you have in mind?"

"I dunno. Something more intimate."

"Hmm," James pretended to give it thought, although in retrospect I think he and his wife had planned this out. They were quite the swingers, we later found out. "I know, how about the guys giving their partner's tits a nice squeeze?"

"Yeah, I like that," said Aaron, pawing at my wife's boobs.

"Wait till he sets the camera," she protested.

"A nice handful," Aaron commented as he took their

measure. Fondling them playfully in his palm.

"Jesus, Aaron. My husband's watching."

James shouted, "Ten seconds!" as he pressed the timer's release.

I reached around to cup Alice's big'uns. They must've weighed ten pounds each. No wonder she needed a heavy-duty brassiere. Those babies had to be backbreakers.

"*Mm-m-m,*" she muttered at my touch.

"Smile!" shouted James.

Z-z-z-z – fl-s-sk!

"Oh my, nobody better see that one," gulped Betsy, quickly removing James' hand from her boobs.

"Surely we can do better than that," said Alice. "Get one of us straddling the guys' laps. Cowgirl position, them sucking on our titties."

"I don't know about that," Barb said, glancing nervously at me.

But I was thinking how much fun it would be to burrow my face against Alice's gigantic mounds. "What the heck," I replied. "Let's try it."

Z-z-z-z – fl-s-sk!

The camera caught me wallowing between Alice's big boobs, Aaron sucking furiously on my wife's tits, and James giving Betsy's nips a sloppy lick.

"Woo," said Barb. Apparently enjoying Aaron's ministrations.

"Hey, you can stop now," I called to him. Aaron seemed to be getting carried away.

"Wait," said James scurrying over to pick up the camera. "Let 'em keep going. This is good stuff."

"Well – " I hesitated.

Fl-s-sk!

"Barb, raise your ass so I can see Aaron's dick. That's it, a little higher."

Fl-s-sk!

"Ooo, it's stiff," my wife commented.

"Like an iron bar," nodded Aaron. "Guess you turn me on."

"I do?"

"Hey, I'd fuck you, if Sam wasn't here –"

"Really?"

"Watch it," I called. Sure that they were kidding.

James had something else in mind. "Barb, how about you position your twat over Aaron's dick. Like you're about to fuck him."

"How's this?" She adjusted her hips.

"Lower. Let the tip of his dick touch you."

"Gee, I dunno about this," she said, but did it anyway.

"A little more. More, more. There, the head's in."

Fl-s-sk!

"I've heard that line before," my wife giggled.

"Then you know what comes next. Squat all way down. Bury that shaft all the way inside you."

To my amazement, my wife complied. Sinking onto Aaron Coulter's thick dick with a lubricated ease. Letting him fuck her in front of the camera. And in front of me.

Fl-s-sk! Fl-s-sk!

"Good, good. Keep going," shouted James. Shooting pictures from all angles. Right, left, up close, from the side.

Barb was rocking up and down on Aaron's member with increasing ferocity. Head thrown back, she was uttering, "*Uh!-uh!-uh!-uh!*" I think she was enjoying it.

Fl-s-sk! Fl-s-sk! Fl-s-sk!

"Great shots." He shifted the camera's angle. "Now Sam, you and Alice."

Without waiting for my response, his wife positioned herself over my stiffie and lowered herself onto it. I could feel the warmth of her interior as my dick slide to its full length. "*Mm-m-m.*" she moaned happily.

"Jesus," I muttered.

"Now me," announced James as he repositioned the camera, set the timer, and raced over to Betsy. She obediently climbed onto his lap, letting him enter her just in time for the camera's shutter.

Z-z-z-z – fl-s-sk!

"Got it. Me fucking Betsy."

"Help yourself," muttered Aaron. Still pounding away at my wife. "I'm busy over here. Barb's got one sweet pussy."

"*Uh*, thanks," she groaned. Not missing a beat. "*Uh!-uh!-uh!*"

"Yeah, thanks," I repeated lamely.

Meanwhile, Alice was bouncing up and down on me, her enormous breasts pummelling my face. I licked and slurped and sucked as we fucked. I felt like I'd landed in the middle of an old Russ Meyer *Supervixens* movie. Bosomania was certainly the word for it!

Betsy was first to cum. Then everybody followed with mews and screams and groans. I felt myself explode inside Alice's loins like a cannon, a blast that lathered her cervix with about a gallon of semen.

As we all uncoupled, I noted Aaron's jism seeping from my wife's pussy, dribbling down her thighs in white, milky rivulets. Thank God she was on the Pill.

James wasn't quite through, forcing his dick in Betsy's mouth, yelling, "Swallow it, swallow it." His cum foaming from between her red lips, dribbling down her chin. Aaron grinned in their direction. Proud that his wife was swallowing without complaint.

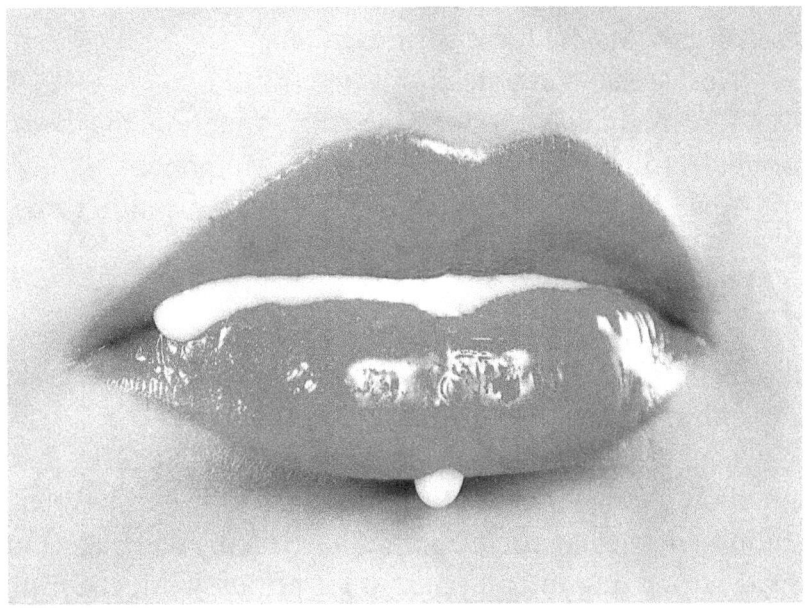

Later, we got dressed in silence, no one willing to talk about what had just happened. An orgy caught on camera. Six friends playing swap-off.

Who would have predicted that when we planned this sunny-day picnic?

I had to admit, Alice had been a great lay, her enthusiasm beyond what I was used to after six sedate years of marriage with Barb. And those big boobs, a bottle baby's dream come true.

"Next time," said James Franklin as he and Alice

dropped us off, "we'll shift. Sam does Betsy, I'll do you Barb, and Aaron gets my wife."

"Mmm, I can't wait," said Barb with a little more eagerness than I'd have liked. She'd been eying James's big dick with interest during the photo shoot. And Betsy had seemed more than satisfied by her coupling with that giant-sized organ. Maybe I was a little jealous.

"Next weekend then?"

"We might have – " I started to mention that we'd promised to visit my parents in nearby Morganton.

"Absolutely," interrupted my wife. "We wouldn't miss it."

"Great."

"And James, see that Sam and I get a set of those pictures," said Barb. "Those pictures will make great souvenirs for our private album. Right, honey?"

"Uh, right," I agreed. Realizing that our lives had somehow changed. Like a tectonic shift in the earth's crust. I didn't know what effect it might have on my marriage, but I was sure going to be getting a lot of pussy. Maybe even another bout with Alice's enormous bazongas.

Like I said, Holy cow!

7

Selena and Mad Dog!

Michael Joseph Morgan was a large hirsute man who wrestled professionally under the name of Mad Dog Mike. Slow moving and not very bright, he was known for his tank-like style in the ring. He made a fearsome visage that sent kids squealing in mock terror.

Born and raised in Axton, Texas, he still lived here with his mother, a frail lady who didn't look big enough to birth a Chihuahua, much less an oversized hair-covered sheepdog.

He suffered from a rare condition known as hypertrichosis. Only about 50 cases of this hair-raising disease have been reported since the Middle Ages. People with congenital hypertrichosis are often referred to as "wolf men," "werewolves" or "ape-men" and have traditionally been crowd-pleasers as sideshow acts. Mike Morgan became a wrestler instead.

He used a dipilitory to keep down the hair, a ritual not unlike weeding a garden. But it grew back in short order. So as not to alarm TV viewers, he was required to wear a body suit and mask like Mexican wrestlers. His costume was quite colorful.

When the Southern Wrestling Conference (SWC) decided to run a series of ads featuring wrestlers posing with gorgeous supermodels – a "Beauty and the Beast" type promotion – Mad Dog Mike requested Selena Mendez. Aside from being a star model in the Ursula's Exotic Undies catalogs, she was a local gal, the girlfriend of his good friend Buddy Miller. When she wasn't off on a photo shoot in New York or Paris, she returned home to Axton.

Truth was, the gentle giant was always mooning after Selena like a lovesick fool. Ever since he'd seen her in those lingerie catalogs, he'd had a permanent hard-on when it came to exotic Mexican women with big boobs.

Selena was thrilled to get the assignment, one that

didn't require her to leave home. She lived with Buddy Miller and his uncle.

Models Unlimited billed her out at $5,000 per day. SWC had hired a famous photographer named Kenneth Kincaid to do the shoot. Selena had posed for him a few years ago when she was barely 18, a neophyte with a small modeling agency in San Antonio. They had a history.

Kenneth was delighted to work with her again. Back when they had first met, she'd posed for some off-the-books photos – fuck pix – that sold very well to the private collectors he supplied in Europe. He was hoping that her current supermodel status wouldn't stand in the way of a repeat performance.

"Interested?" he put it to her when they discussed the assignment.

"Maybe," she allowed. She wasn't sexually shy. And she knew her boyfriend would never see them, the customers being a few European counts and wealthy businessmen.

"That-a girl."

"Who would I be posing with?"

"How about Mad Dog Mike?"

"I beg your pardon?"

"I said, how about Mad Dog Mike? You know, some erotic pictures of you with the wrestler. That'd be kinky."

"Has Mad Dog agreed?"

"Don't think that'll be a problem."

"Why's that?"

Kenneth chuckled. "Look in a mirror, sweetheart. He won't say *no*."

The idea of posing for fuck photographs with Mike Morgan was intriguing to Selena. With his hairy pelt, it was as close to bestiality as she'd likely ever come. The resulting photos would be a classic Beauty and the Beast homage, with her playing a sexually explicit Fay Wray to his King Kong. She could hardly wait.

She wondered if his dick matched his oversized physique.

~ ~ ~

Mad Dog Mike opened the front door of the sprawling ranchhouse where he lived with his mother and greeted Selena and the photo crew with a wide grin. "As I live an' breathe, it's one-a my favorite people in the whole wide world. Howdy, Miss Selena."

"Hi, Mad Dog. Thanks for requesting me for your SWC ad."

"My pleasure," he nodded. The big wrestler could barely keep his eyes off Selena, her standing there in a tight blue T and short shorts. The prophetic words on the cotton T-shirt said WHIP ME, BEAT ME, FUCK ME, TREAT ME LIKE THE WHORE I AM. Fortunately (or perhaps unfortunately depending on your point of view) Mad Dog was functionally illiterate and didn't get the message.

"This is Kenneth Kincaid, the photographer who's going to shoot today's pictures. And these other two guys are his photo crew. Madeleine here is the makeup artist. It's her job to make you and me look good."

"That's gonna be a tall order with me," he winked. "And, sweet thing, you don't need no improvement."

"Silly boy."

"Howdy, folks," the wrestler turned to the others. "Pleased t' meet you all."

Kincaid nodded. "Mr. Morgan, it's indeed a pleasure."

"Glad you was willing to do the photos here at my farm. Don't like to travel 'less I'm on the wrestling circuit."

"Where's your mom?" Selena asked, glancing around the living room. The couch and easy chair were protected by plastic slipcases, the lampshades still covered in cellophane. Knickknack shelves displayed Hummel figurines. A black velvet painting of The Last Supper hung over the couch like a religious shrine.

"She went over to console Frannie Richards. Rubberneck's in jail y' know."

"Heard you were too."

"Only overnight. Sheriff Tilton released me on my own recognizance. As you probably you know, the sheriff's wife was a Morgan 'fore they got married."

"So was Rubberneck's wife Frannie."

"Yeah, but Frannie don't want Rubberneck back home 'til he dries out. He tends to be a mean drunk."

"What did you do?" asked Kincaid. Fascinated by this monster of a man.

"Best I remember we got in a fight with Buster Davis an' his gang down at Sally's Sarsaparilla Saloon."

"I heard Buster's in the hospital in Austin," said Selena. "A broken clavicle."

"I broke his clavicle? I didn't even know he played a musical instrument."

Selena rolled her eyes, reminding herself that she was only going to have sex with the big dummy, not bear his children.

"Perhaps we should get started," suggested Kenneth Kincaid. "We want to finish these pictures before your mother gets home – so as not to inconvenience her."

"Sure thing. We can take 'em down in the barn if you like. I got a wrestling ring set up there so's I can practice my moves."

Selena and the camera crew followed Mad Dog down the graveled path to a large red barn. Turns out he was wearing his tights under the bib overalls, having anticipated their arrival. When he shucked his outer clothing, he looked like that character Chewbacca in *Star Wars*. More hair than skin showing.

"Holy shit!" said Selena in spite of herself.

Kincaid gave her a stern look, afraid she'd queer the deal. He'd heard the big wrestler was sensitive about his appearance.

"I mean, what big muscles you have," Selena corrected herself.

"Thank you. I try t' keep in shape." He proceeded to use a liquid depilatory to wipe away huge patches of hair, working at it until his chest was bare. "There," he said, "now I look a l'il more human."

"You look quite handsome," she lied.

"Aw shucks." He beamed ear-to-ear.

The two assistants set up the lights and a tripod supporting a motorized Nikon. Madeleine applied eyeliner and blush to Selena's countenance, added lipstick.

The big wrestler watched. "Gee, Miss Selena, you sure do look pretty," he said with the tone of a lovesick suitor. He was a hopeless case when it came to the Mexican beauty.

"Thanks, Mad Dog."

Kenneth Kincaid smiled. This would be like taking candy from a baby. Mad Dog Mike obviously had a crush on Selena Mendez.

For the next three hours he took photographs for the SWC ad campaign. Mad Dog in his wrestling tights; Selena in shorts and a striped referee's shirt that was tied off to create a bare midriff. The wrestler growling at the camera and flexing his muscles while Selena looked pretty.

They were quite the mismatched twosome: Selena tall at 5' 10"; the wrestler a good eight inches taller. Mutt and Jeff.

Fl-s-s-k! Fl-s-s-k! and *Fl-s-s-k!*

"Those were nice photos," allowed Kenneth Kincaid as he wrapped up the shoot.

"Didja get what you wanted?" asked Mad Dog.

"Yes. I think SWC will be very happy with the results."

"That's grrrrreat!" He did his Tony the Tiger imitation. Sounding more like a wounded bobcat.

"Before we wrap up, what say we get a few risqué pictures of you and Selena. Just for fun."

"Risky?"

"Sexy," Selena explained. "Like those picture of me in the lingerie catalogs."

"You mean you in your underwear?"

"Maybe less clothes than that."

"Less?"

"Like naked."

"Oh boy. You naked. I can't wait to see them big titties."

Kincaid nodded jovially. "Selena, if that's what Mad Dog wants, why don't you start by taking off that referee's shirt?"

"Sure," she said. Pulling the cotton garment over her head, dragging her boobs upward with the tight fabric, causing them to bounce as she freed her dark hair.

Mad Dog's eyes bulged. "Good God Almighty, look-a that. Your titties are big as melons, Miss Selena."

"So they are," she purred.

"Am I gonna get t' touch 'em?" asked Mad Dog.

"More than that."

"More?"

"We're going to make some Tijuana Bible pictures," she explained.

"You mean I get t' fuck you?"

Selena glanced at the photographer, catching his nod. "Absolutely," she affirmed.

"Oh boy. I been wanting t' do that for a long time. Ever since I saw you in that lingerie catalog." Her appearance in Ursula's Erotic Undies had been quite a scandal in Axton.

"Then this is your lucky day."

Mad Dog hesitated. "You sure your boyfriend's all right with this?"

"You can't tell Buddy about this. It has to be our secret."

"Oh."

"He might get jealous, me fucking one of his friends."

"I don't wanna piss Buddy off."

"Relax. He'll never know," she smiled.

"First, let's get a photo of Mad Dog playing with your titties," suggested the photographer.

Mad Dog Mike was happy to oblige. Grasping her bazooms in his big mitts. His palms easily covering them despite their C-cup size.

Fl-s-s-k!

For the next shot Mad Dog pretended to trap Selena in a bear hug, towering behind her like a Giant Kodiak, his muscular arms wrapped around her torso, the bare breasts resting on his locked forearms.

Selena smiled seductively into the Nikor lens. "Cheese," she said, more as a joke than a way of showing her pearly whites in the photo. Being a professional model, she knew how to turn it on for a photograph, her sensuality practically scorching the camera's SIM card.

Fl-s-s-k! Fl-s-s-k!

"Rubberneck's sure gonna be sorry he wasn't here t' see this." The little lowlife was Mad Dog Mike's best friend. The two had palled around since grade school; Rubberneck being the brains and Mad Dog the muscle. Sort of an *Of Mice and Men* relationship.

"Hold on, you can't tell Roger about this either," Selena cautioned as she wiggled out of her short shorts. The exertion caused her breasts to bounce again. But the wrestler's eyes were locked on her exposed pubes.

"Whoa, Miss Selena, I can see your puss."

"Like it?"

"I'll say."

"Now you."

"Me?"

"Mr. Kincaid's gonna get some pictures of us doing the Dirty Deed. You have to take off those tights if you want to fuck me."

"Let's get to the hardcore action," Kincaid announced as he put in a fresh SIM card. "These are gonna be a great set of pictures. Beauty and the Beast."

"Which one am I?" asked the simple giant.

"Guess," giggled Selena.

She struck a sultry pose in the corner of the ring. The big wrestler lumbered over to join her.

"Okay, Mad Dog, start off by nibbling on her tits," instructed Kenneth Kincaid as he focus the camera.

"Yummy," said the wrestler as he applied his mouth to her pointy brown nips. Like a kid savoring nougaty Sugar Babies.

"*Mm-m*," Selena responded. "Bite harder."

"You sure?"

"I like rough sex."

Fl-s-s-k!

"Okay, Selena, fuck him."

"My pleasure." Placing her back against the turnbuckle, she wrapped her arms around the top rope and swung upward to scissor her legs around the big man's hips. "Do it," she whispered.

The big man pushed his way inside her. "Lord have mercy," he muttered, eyes rolling back in his head. His winkie was actually *inside* Selena Mendez, the prettiest gal in the whole damn county. Who woulda thought he'd ever be doing this?

"*Mm-m-m*," she accepted the bodily intrusion. "That feels good."

"I'll say."

"Get a picture of this," she said to Kincaid. "Me getting fucked by the man who once won the belt from Hulk Hogan."

Fl-s-s-k! – The photographer got the shot. He was surprised she knew so much about wrestling championships.

"Put it all way inside me," she instructed her partner.

"It is all way in," he insisted.

"Ram it home."

"Uh, okay." His hips were like a pile driver. Each trust slammed her against the turnbuckle.

"Get a shot of his dick inside me," she said to the photographer. As if she were directing the photo shoot.

Fl-s-s-k! – Kincaid obliged with a close-up. The visual equivalency to a Pig In A Blanket: a stubby wiener wrapped in a golden brown pastry. He was pleased with the way the shoot was going. The spectacle of this monster ravishing a beautiful model was something you'd never see outside of a carnival freak show. His collectors would be ecstatic with these images.

Fl-s-s-k!

"That's it, fuck me harder," she whispered in a husky voice.

"Can I cum inside you, Miss Selena?" the wrestler asked with the naïveté of a child.

"I don't mind," she said, her breath coming in ragged gasps. "But hold off a bit longer if you can. I want to get off first."

"Don't rightly think I can do that," he said as Selena felt the twitchy spasms of his orgasm.

"Mad Dog – !"

"Hope you ain't mad at me."

"That's all right," she sighed. Feeling his spunk drip down her inner thighs.

Fl-s-s-k!

Mad Dog's hands were still supporting her butt, hoisting her off the canvas as he continued banging her. But she could tell his stiffie was starting to flag. Damn!

"Selena, go down on him," suggested Kincaid. Not willing to call it quits yet. "Maybe you can get him stiff again."

"I'll do my best," she said, wiggling out of the big man's clutches, feet touching the floor. "One Grade-A blowjob coming up."

"*Eiiik-k-k!*" – a cry punctuated the stillness inside the barn.

Mad Dog looked around. "Mom?" he said. "Whatcha doin' home so early?"

"Mikey Joe Morgan, what'n tarnation do you think you're doing up there with that naked woman?"

Selena picked up her T-shirt and held it discretely in front of her bare skin. "Hi, Mrs. Morgan. It's just me – Selena Mendez. Buddy Miller's girlfriend."

Mad Dog Mike might be semi-literate, but his mother could obviously read. Her mouth dropped open as she made out the message on the blue cotton background: WHIP ME, BEAT ME, FUCK ME, TREAT ME LIKE THE WHORE I AM. "Well, as I live an' breathe," the old woman croaked, eyes bulging at the sight.

"Oops," said Selena, reversing the T-shirt front to back. Flashing her audience in the process.

This audience consisted of three elderly ladies: Minnie Morgan, Mad Dog Mike's bird-like mother. Myrtle Longbottom, a local dowager whose late husband had surveyed most of the county. And Evangeline Alberta Swinton, the witch woman who lived across the mountain. Vangie to her friends, not that she had many. Holy moley! – a more intimidating threesome couldn't be found outside of Act IV Scene I in *Macbeth*.

"Selena Mendez, may I ask what you're doing naked as a jaybird with my son? Let me tell you, Buddy's Uncle Pete is certainly going to hear about this!"

Kenneth Kincaid offered his best smile. "Mrs. Morgan, there's a simple explanation for all this – " he began.

"This I gotta hear," scoffed Myrtle Longbottom. A confirmed skeptic, she would argue over the color of a blue sky. "Looks to me like some kinda orgy going on here."

"Let him speak," said Minnie Morgan. Looking for answers. The women had been calling on Frannie Richards, Rubberneck's wife. And no one was prepared to encounter this scene of licentious debauchery in the Morgans' big red barn.

The photographer cleared his throat. "Selena was helping your son practice some new wrestling moves. The SWC is planning some mixed matches, men an' women together. To practice the moves, they have to strip down naked to achieve maximum mobility. These are very tricky holds."

"And what are you doing with that camera?"

"We photograph each practice session to make sure he's got the holds right," Kincaid improvised. "Right, fellows?"

"That's right," echoed his first assistant. The lighting guy and makeup artist nodded in unison. "Right!" "Uh-huh."

Minnie Morgan eyed her son with a steely gaze. "Is that true, Mikey Joe?"

Mad Dog knew when he was boxed into a corner, the only escape being to lie like a sonuvabitch. So he blurted: "Yessum, that's exactly what we're doin' here. Practicing for my next match. I'm scheduled t' go up against Shawna the Jungle Girl. She's as limber as a cat. Beatin' her's gonna require lotsa practice."

"Oh, well, that explains it." Mad Dog Mike's mother was quick to accept her son's claim of purity despite all evidence to the contrary.

Myrtle Longbottom didn't look convinced, however she kept her mouth shut. Vangie Swinton spoke up to say they ought not be interrupting professionals at work.

Mrs. Morgan beamed at this description of her dimwitted son as a "professional." She sometimes worried that his wrestling job was only slightly higher on the occupational scale than that of a circus clown. "Yes, let's get back to the house. It's time for our stories." The women never missed their television soap operas if they could help it. *As The World Turns* was the favorite, with *My Life Is My Own* running a close second.

"Okay, for this next move Selena's gonna jump off the top rope and hit Mad Dog with a body slam," Kenneth Kincaid was saying in a deep stage voice as the three women hobbled up the path toward the farmhouse.

"Je-sus!" said Selena when they were out of hearing. "I can't believe Mad Dog's mom practically caught me fucking him." She tossed her T-shirt in the air as if giving up on the fairness of life.

"Better get your clothes on," Kincaid told them. "Show's over."

"Did you get some good photos for your collectors?" she inquired while climbing out of the ring to retrieve her T-shirt and shorts.

"Yes indeed." He tilted his head to study her. "Are you okay?"

She sighed. "I'm still high and dry. Making it with Mad Dog's akin to getting fucked by an overeager cocker spaniel."

"What about my cock – ?" Mad Dog was stepping into his bib overalls, fastening the galluses.

"A very fine cock," Selena assured him. "I can attest to that fact."

"Thank you kindly, Miss Selena. I never thought I'd get a chance t' fuck a pretty lady like you."

"Life is full of surprises."

"Y' think I might get surprised again sometime?"

"We'll see," she put him off. A bit disgruntled by the lack of orgasm.

"Rubberneck ain't gonna believe this," mused the big wrestler. "Me fucking you an' my mom walks in. Ain't that a hoot?"

"No, no," she admonished. "This is our little secret, remember? You can't tell anybody about this. Especially not Rubberneck Richards. Or my boyfriend Buddy."

"Ain't gonna be much of a secret if my mom an' her garden-club friends know about it."

"They think you're practicing some fancy wrestling moves," Kincaid reminded him.

"Oh yeah, right. You sure pulled the fat outta the fire with that one."

"Yes, quick thinking," Selena agreed.

"You dressed yet, Selena? We'd best be going."

"Just about."

He noted she'd put her T-shirt on inside-out so the words wouldn't show. She was looking for one of her slippers. "Over there, under the edge of the ring," he pointed. You could still see the streaks of Mad Dog's semen on the inside of her brown thighs.

"Thanks."

"Mr. Morgan, do you mind signing this model's release," said the first assistant. "A mere formality."

"Is this release for the promotion pictures. Or the ones of me fucking Miss Selena?"

"Both."

"Dunno if the SWC would want me okaying fuck pictures," he hesitated.

"Sign it and I'll let you do me again next week," coaxed Selena. Regretting her words as she said them.

"No shit? That's a deal." He scribbled his name on the release, a series of chicken-scratch X's.

"Bye, Mad Dog. Our secret, remember?"

"Yessum. Can't wait t' see the pictures."

"She'll have proofs tomorrow," Kenneth Kincaid promised.

"Oh boy."

As they climbed into the van, she said, "You know he'll talk."

"Any guy would. Who could fuck you and not wanna brag about it?"

"You for one."

"May I remind you I'm gay."

"Oh, right."

~ ~ ~

Later that day Myrtle Longbottom caught up with her at the Winn-Dixie. Axton only had one supermarket, so it had become something of a social center. "Selena Mendez, you may have fooled Minnie but you can't fool me. I've asked Reverend Smithy to pray for your immortal soul." Myrtle was leader of the Women's Auxiliary at Holy Spirit Baptist Church.

"Thank you. I can use all the help I can get."

"The very nerve, having sexual congress with that big halfwit. What will your boyfriend think?"

"Uh – "

"Word's gonna be out on you, Selena"

"Don't be so quick t' judge, Myrtle," said a voice from the back of the store. It caught both women by surprise.

"Who – ?"

Uncle Pete stepped from behind the canned goods aisle. He was manager of the Axton Winn-Dixie. "You spread word on that girl an' I might have t' speak up 'bout that weekend you spent with me back in '76 while your husband was surveying over in Pecos county."

"You wouldn't dare – "

"As I recall, *you* did dare," the man grinned at the memory. "Gotta admit you were a hot piece of ass in your day, Myrtle."

"*Ahem*, perhaps we should let sleeping dogs lie. You keep our secrets and I'll keep Selena's. Agreed?"

Pete Miller nodded his accord. "Always a pleasure t' see you, Myrtle."

~ ~ ~

"You owe me one," said Buddy's uncle. A grin splitting his broad face.

"Guess I do, at that. How do you want to collect?" Letting the options lie there unspoken.

Pete chuckled at her remark. "Ain't a question of how. Only a question of when."

"You tease. You wouldn't be flirting with me if Buddy were here to hear you."

"Hm, don't think you want him knowing about that photo session with Mike Morgan. That true?"

"Maybe it should stay between us."

"Can I have a peek the pictures? I'd like to see you havin' some hot-pillow action. Bet you'd be a regular Jenna Jameson."

"Not quite. My skin is brown. And my boobs are real."

He eyed her chest. "Yes ma'am, I'd bet your tits are a sight t' behold. Now about them pictures, you gonna show 'em to me?"

"Maybe."

"That-a girl."

~ ~ ~

Mad Dog Mike Morgan came by the house that next afternoon before she'd had a chance to show the photos to Uncle Pete. Oh well, first come, first serve.

"Hey there, Miss Selena. My mom said t' tell you hello. She 'preciates you helping me practice my wrestling moves."

"My pleasure – literally." Wrestling moves indeed!

"Can't wait t' do it again. Even if nobody believes me 'bout fuckin' you."

"*Je-sus!* You weren't supposed to tell anyone," she reminded him. She poured him a cup of coffee and placed it on the dinette table, an invitation for him to sit.

"Don't worry, I didn't tell a soul 'cept Rubberneck. Oh yeah, I mighta mentioned it t' Butterball an' his cousin Leo. An' maybe Pablo Hernandez, that's Suzy's brother. He's back from Afghanistan. But nobody else."

Holy moley! Mad Dog may as well have taken out a full-page ad in the *Axton Chronicle*. Hopefully, everyone would assume the dimwitted giant was having another one of his fantasies. Last year he swore he'd seen pixies picking mushrooms down at Loon Lake.

"Here, look at this," she slid a stack of photographs across the table. A sly smile as she submitted this evidence of their carnality.

The hairy man bent over the top 4" x 6" glossy, squinting to study the image:

> *Him supporting Selena Mendez's*
> *naked brown butt as he screwed*
> *her in the corner of the ring.*

He turned to the next photograph in the stack:

A close up of his stubby organ buried in her snatch. Every detail in ultra-sharp focus.

Mad Dog certainly liked them. "Heck, Miss Selena, you oughta put these pictures in your next catalog. All my buddies would sure like to see 'em."

"Can't do that."

"Why not?"

"Because it's a lingerie catalog. I'm naked in these photos."

"Oh, right."

"Besides, we can't let Buddy know about these photos."

"Got it. He might see 'em if they was in the catalog."

"About that return match – " She was trying to think of a way to back out of screwing him again.

"My mom's going t' visit her sister in Houston this weekend. Why don't you come over on Saturday an' we'll do it again. I'll invite Rubberneck an' some of the guys to watch. Bet we could get us a good audience."

"Hold on, Mad Dog. This isn't a SWC wrestling match. Our little tryst is supposed to be a secret."

"Sorry."

She slid the photographs into a drawer, signaling the subject was closed. "We'll discuss this later," she said.

~ ~ ~

Selena plopped the photos down on the kitchen table where Uncle Pete was reading a newsletter called *UFO Hotline.* He was convinced that earth was being visited by aliens from the dog star Sirius. "You wanted to see these, I believe," she said.

Pete laid the newsletter aside and turned his attention to the proffered photos. "Are these the ones you told me about?"

"Uh-huh. Pictures of me having sex with Mad Dog Mike."

"Well, I'll be danged," Pete said as he examined the photograph on top:

> *Selena with freaky Mike Morgan, him banging her in a corner of a wrestling ring. Like an X-rated version of a SWC grudge match.*

"Heavens to Betsy, girl. These are the hottest pictures I ever seen."

"Thank you."

"I gotta give 'em back?"

"Yes, I can't have Buddy's coming across them."

He furrowed his brow. "So why are you showing 'em t' me? These *are* a mite personal."

"You said you wanted to see them. You calmed down Myrtle Longbottom. I figured I owed you this much."

"Maybe more," Uncle Pete said as he examined the next photograph in the stack. "Think I'd like t' fuck you too."

Selena Mendez shrugged. "Sure," she said. "Why not? Anytime you like, except for next weekend. I'm already booked on Saturday."

8
Making A Porn Video

Archie picked up the car keys from the shelf next to the door and announced, "I'm goin' out for a spell. Gotta see a man 'bout a dog." He and his wife and a few friends had rented a summerhouse on Lake Lure, practically in the shadow of Chimney Rock. Or Cock Rock, as his wife liked to refer to the phallus-shaped rock formation that's now a state park.

"Please don't take too long, dear," called Annie. "We're going to watch a movie later on the DVD player."

"Which one?"

"When we went to Ingle's yesterday, Pinkie picked up *Hello, Dolly!*" Annie replied. "A Barbra Streisand musical."

"Aw, that's cruel an' unusual punishment."

"You were hoping for *Debbie Does Dallas*?"

"How 'bout *Debbie Does Asheville*?" rejoined her husband. "I'd like to see that li'l gal get around more."

"Maybe we should make our own home movie," Annie suggested mischievously. "I could pretend to be Little Red Riding Hood and you be the Big Bad Wolf?"

"Don't think I'm ready for the silver screen," Archie said to his wife. He tended to be camera shy. Poor self-image or some such.

"Spoilsport."

"Y'all go ahead an' watch *Hello, Dolly!* Don't bother waitin' f' me," he said jangling the car keys. "I'll be back by lunch."

"We'll do hamburgers on the grill outside," she said.

"Sounds good." Up from Charlotte for the month, Archie Andrews -- yes, he had the same name as that comic book character -- along with his wife and four friends were enjoying the cool mountain breezes.

"You don't want to be in an X-rated video with me?" pouted Annie. "Guess we'll have to do it without you."

"Go to it," he winked.

"Might be fun," she said.

"Are you serious?" asked Big Dog Blankenship. Batting his eyes in confusion. "You'd actually do an X-rated video, Annie Andrews?"

"Why not?"

"You're talking actual fuckin' an' suckin' – right?" said Jimmy John Jackson. A big grin crossing her face.

Annie appraised her husband's miscreant friends. "Are you saying you boys would like to watch me perform hardcore sex acts?"

"You bet your sweet ass we would."

"Don't worry. If I ever do a video I promise you won't be disappointed."

"Hot damn. I can't wait."

Ruthie Stinson giggled. She was Annie's official BFF. "Can I be in your home movie? I've always wanted to be eaten by a Big Bad Wolf!"

"But Archie said he didn't want t' be in the video," Big Dog pointed out. Clearly disappointed.

"Maybe you could play the Wolf if Archie doesn't want

to do it," teased Ruthie. "You're certainly hairy enough."

"Yes," giggled Annie. "And you already have the name. A wolf is just a big dog."

"I'd be willing t' stand in for Archie," nodded the giant. "That is, if I got t' fuck you, Annie."

"Bill Blankenship!"

"Just being honest."

"Hey, can I be in this movie too?" said Jimmy John Jackson.

"Get in line," laughed Archie. "She's got lots of guys lustin' after her ahead of you good ol' boys."

Annie smiled wistfully. "I have to admit making a porno video would be more fun than watching a rerun of *Hello, Dolly!* And since we don't have anybody else here today, I supposed we'd have to use the talent available."

"That would be us," Big Dog nodded eagerly. "We're available – right, Jimmy John?"

"You bet," said his pal. "An' I got acting experience. I was in a play in the third grade."

"An adult video has certain physical requirements," observed Annie. "I doubt you had sex with anybody in that third grade play."

"No, but I fucked my seventh grade teacher. Does that count?"

"How old were you?"

"Fifteen. I'd been held back a coupla years."

"You had sex with a grown woman when you were fifteen?"

"Right there on her desk after school. Musta done a good job of it. She gave me an A-plus in Phys Ed."

Big Dog nodded. "I remember her – Mrs. Rayburn."

"She had nice tits," nodded Jimmy John.

"Dis-*gust*-ing," groaned Annie's friend Pinkie. He had delicate sensibilities.

"Hmm, you might have the right talent for a porn movie after all," allowed Annie.

"That I can guarantee you," bragged Jimmy John.

"Would you be willing to audition for the part?"

"You mean show you my dick? No problem."

"Don't unzip your pants."

"Anytime you wanna inspect it, just say the word."

"I'll keep that in mind."

Archie shook his head in amusement. Let his wife feed their fantasies, those horny idiots. Like anything was really gonna happen. "While y'all plan this epic production, I'm off to Hendersonville. Anything you girls need?"

"Would you mind picking up some more limes?" said Ruthie, trying to suppress her laughter. The idea of a porn video was a hoot. "We're running low after that last batch of kamikazes."

"That's all?"

"Oh, maybe that cute cop – Lieutenant Hendricks."

"Sorry, Ruthie. I draw the line at pimpin' for you."

"He could be in the video with us." A Hendersonville cop named Benny Hendricks had pulled Ruthie over for running a stop sign and they had hit up a conversation. Turns out, he didn't give her a ticket but he did write his phone number on the back of the warning.

"Ask him yourself," said Archie.

"Spoilsport!"

"People keep calling me that."

"With good reason," she replied.

Archie stepped through the door onto the shaded porch. "See y'all later," he called over his shoulder to Annie and his friends.

"No need to hurry, dear. We'll figure out something to occupy us while you're gone. Maybe Ruthie will loan us her video camera."

"Have fun," Archie said. He was pretty sure she was kidding.

≈≈≈

Archie – short for Archimedes – drove into Hendersonville to meet with a man who had a restored Austin Healy Sprite for sale. A 1961 bugeyed model. He'd always wanted one.

He'd located the car through his pal Big Dog. Bill Blankenship was a prominent car dealer in Charlotte, known for his corny TV ads ("Buy your next Buick from the Big Dog!"). Jimmy John was head of Blankenship Buick's service department. The three of them – Archie, Big Dog and Jimmy John – had been best buddies since the third grade at Winget Park Elementary. *Go Winget Wolves!*

Wasn't much he wouldn't share with his two buds. Like this summer rental on Lake Lure. Big Dog was single, and Jimmy John was always looking for an excuse to get away from his wife. Ruthie and Pinkie were Archie's wife's additions. Everybody was a little hesitant to invite Pinkie, but he worked for Annie at All American Insurance so they made an exception. Maybe just to prove they weren't homophobic.

≈≈≈

Back at the summer house, Pinkie Pitney was trying to talk everybody into watching *Hello, Dolly!*, his very favorite

Barbra Streisand movie.

Jimmy John and Big Dog were objecting strenuously, holding out for *Rambo*.

An impasse.

Ruthie broke the tie when she said, "I'm surprised you boys aren't trying to talk Annie into making that porn video. She might just do it while Archie's not here."

Annie looked up from the latest issue of *Southern Living*. "Ruthie, quit causing trouble," she said. "These horny rednecks are going to take you seriously."

"Well, you *did* promise them," said her girlfriend. "I've got a Canon FV30 digital camcorder with a 22x optical zoom, if you want to borrow it."

"Thanks, Ruthie. You're very helpful," her girlfriend said, not meaning it] at all.

Big Dog spoke up. "C'mon, Miss Annie, you promised."

"Hey, that's right," Jimmy John weighed in. "You offered to star in a racy video."

"I did not."

Ruthie smiled impishly. "You've got to admit making a racy video would be a lot more fun than watching another Barbra Streisand movie."

"Got that right," said Jimmy John Jackson. Yesterday Pinkie had forced them to sit through *Yentl*, quite an ordeal for two plainspoken Southern boys.

"Hey!" protested Pinkie. "You're saying you had rather see Annie naked than watch a classic Barbra Streisand musical?"

"Hell, yes!" exclaimed Jimmy John.

"Ain't no contest," grinned Big Dog.

"Boys, I'm flattered." Annie smiled at the two salivating

men. "But really –"

Pinkie had to concede that it was a toss-up between Streisand and Annie Andrews in his pantheon of goddesses. He worshipped his supervisor at the insurance company, the way a teenager moons over a movie star. "I suppose we can watch *Hello, Dolly!* any ol' time," he said. "And it's not every day that our Annie agrees to make an X-rated movie."

"I haven't agreed," she corrected him.

"But you will," said Ruthie. "You're such a show-off."

"I have to admit I've always wanted to do an X-rated video," Annie giggled. "But Archie doesn't like to be on camera. Even refuses to get his picture taken."

"So make one with us," said Big Dog. "Me and Jimmy John ain't shy."

"Our own little production," mused Pinkie, usually the prude. "It would be fun to see what we could come up with."

"Count me in," said Ruthie. "I'm game."

Annie tossed her magazine aside. "Do you think I should do it?" she addressed Pinkie – her unofficial consigliore.

"It would be terribly naughty. But we'd all enjoy seeing your debut as a porn star, my dear."

"I'm tempted," she admitted.

"It would be just among friends," coaxed Ruthie. "Nobody would ever know. Not even Archie."

"Hmm . . ."

"I've always wanted to direct a movie," declared Pinkie Pitney. His true motivation coming out. "I can help with the script and makeup. Oh, and I can be the cameraman too. Don't worry about a thing, Annie dear. All you'd have to do is look beautiful."

"An' get naked," Big Dog prompted.

"An' fuck like a bunny," Jimmy John amended.

Annie hesitated. "If I *did* agree to do an adult video you'd have to promise nobody else would ever see it – especially Archie."

"I promise not to tell," said Big Dog.

"That's right. Nobody would know 'bout this 'cept us," nodded Jimmy John. Raising his hand as if taking an oath.

"Couldn't I show it to Benny?" asked Ruthie. "I know he'd want to see the movie if I were in it."

"Perhaps he could have a part," suggested Annie. "I wouldn't mind doing your cop boyfriend. He's kinda cute."

"Hey, you won't let me do your husband. So why should I share my new beau?"

"Maybe we could work out a reciprocal trade," teased Annie.

"Fat chance of that. Archie's too straight-laced to do a swap."

"True. But what about making Benny the star of our video?"

"No, better not. Being a member of the law enforcement community, he could lose his job if he got caught appearing in a porno."

"Then who would I perform with?"

"Perform with?" said Jimmy John. "You mean fuck, don'tcha?"

"I was thinking Soft X," negotiated Annie Andrews. "You know, simulated sex."

"You mean jus' pretend?" said Big Dog. Frowning, not liking the idea.

"You said we wouldn't be disappointed in your

performance," Jimmy John reminded her. "An' I'd surely be disappointed with anything less from you than down-an'-dirty moanin'-an'-groanin' cum-splattered fuckin' an' suckin'."

"Don't be so shy about saying what you really want to see," responded Annie. Fascinated by her husband's friends' interest in fucking her.

"That was the whole idear," said Jimmy John, "seein' you carryin' on like a real porn star."

"Yes, but –"

"Chicken!" chided Ruthie. "I'll do it if you will."

"You'd do hardcore?"

"Why do something halfway?" said the blonde. Being twice divorced, Ruthie was fairly free with her favors.

"But who would we fuck?" posited Annie Andrews. "One of these lowlifes?" She waved her hand to take in Big Dog and Jimmy John. "Surely you're not serious. These are my husband's best friends."

"Better his friends than his enemies," Pinkie said philosophically.

"What's wrong with us?" whined Jimmy John, a man known to have a perpetual hard-on. "I'd fuck both-a you gals in a heartbeat."

"That fast?" taunted Annie. "No wonder your wife doesn't mind you being away from home so much."

"Betty Sue ain't got no complaints about her sex life. I keep that woman happier'n a clover-fed heifer. She's the love o' my life."

"Then why do you want to fuck li'l ol' me?" Annie put on a show of innocence. Head cocked, a finger to her pouty lips. Never mind that her blouse was unbuttoned low enough to show the swell of her breasts.

"Damn, Annie Andrews, ain't you never looked in the mirror? Even the devil himself would wanna bed you."

"And you're quite the devil," she winked at Jimmy John Jackson.

"What about me?" sulked Big Dog Blankenship. "I been dreaming 'bout fuckin' you ever since Archie brought you home from Indiana. I ain't never had me no Yankee before."

"A Yankee comes from the North; Indiana's in the Midwest," corrected Annie. "I'm what they call a Hoosier."

"A who?"

"Hoosier."

"Whatever the heck you are, I'd still like to do you."

"Thank you, Big Dog. That's sweet of you to say."

"So can I be in the video with you?" begged the big man. "I won't tell Archie you let me fuck you."

"That's right," said Jimmy John. "Nary a word. Being Archie's our friend, we wouldn't wanna rub his nose in it."

"How considerate," laughed Ruthie. "You'd fuck his wife as long as it's behind his back."

"Common courtesy," mumbled Jimmy John.

"Boys –" Annie began to backpedal. "I can't be having sex with you. It just wouldn't be right, a married woman fooling around with her husband's best friends."

"Oh hush," said Ruthie. "You know you're going to fuck them both once the camera gets rolling."

"What makes you say that, Miss Know-It-All?"

"Because I've known you since college. You fucked every boy in the senior class."

"I quit my slutty ways after I married Archie."

"But you make exceptions," her girlfriend pointed out. "I recall that vacuum cleaner salesman last Spring –"

"He gave me $40 off on a new Electrolux."

"And that lifeguard at the Y –"

"He *was* awfully cute."

"I rest my case."

Annie shrugged. "Okay, you talked me into it."

"Then it's settled," said Pinkie. "We're making a porno movie."

"You sure you don't want to be in it?" encouraged Ruthie Stinson. "It's not every day you get a chance to fuck your boss."

"Would it get me a raise?"

"Not a chance," laughed Annie. "But I give a great blowjob."

"Oh my, I could never have sex with a woman," Pinkie rolled his eyes. "Not even with you, Annie. But I'd be delighted to operate the camera while the four of you copulate like minks."

"Pinkie, you're rejecting me," Annie teased. "My heart is broken."

The rotund man shrugged. "I predict these two scoundrels will be quite adequate for your purposes."

"There's one way to find," smiled Annie. "Let's do a screen test."

Big Dog grinned. "You mean you'll fuck us?"

"No promises. But I'll get naked. You boys would like that, wouldn't you?"

"That's a start," acknowledged Jimmy John.

"I've always wanted t' see your titties," nodded Big Dog.

"Oh, you'll get to see more than that," Annie assured him, throwing caution to the winds. The thought of appearing in a sex video was making hormones rage through her nether regions like a tsunami.

"Let me go get my video camera," said Ruthie.

Moments later she returned from the rec room with the

Canon FV30 camcorder and handed it over to Pinkie. "Do you know how to work one of these?"

"I can do *anything*," said the little man. Already fiddling with the settings.

"Don't break it."

"Break what?" said Annie.

"Your hymen," quipped Ruthie.

"Oh, I lost that in college."

"To the history professor, as I recall."

"I was going for extra credits."

"Let's get started," interjected Pinkie. "Better hurry if you want to get this done before Archie gets back." He glanced at his Fossil wristwatch. "It's now ten o'clock. That gives us two hours."

Ruthie rolled her eyes. "As if these guys could actually last two hours with us."

Annie shrugged. "Okay, you talked me into it." She glanced out the picture window overlooking the lake. The sky was overcast. It was starting to sprinkle, water droplets pocking the surface of the lake. "What better to do on a rainy day than make a porn movie?"

"First, we need a storyline," suggested Pinkie.

"I thought we were doing *Little Red Riding Hood*," said Annie.

"Boring."

"Given the cast we have to work with," said Ruthie, "how about *Beauty and the Beast*. Annie is of course Beauty. And Big Dog makes the perfect Beast."

"Hey, that's typecasting," he said.

"Do you want to fuck Annie or not?" responded Ruthie.

"*Growl*," he said. "I'm the Beast."

"What about me?" said Jimmy John. "I wanna fuck 'er too."

Pinkie took charge. "You get to copulate with Ruthie. Then we'll do a mix-and-match-em for the finale."

"Well, okay." Truth is, Jimmy John Jackson had been lusting after Annie's girlfriend all week. He had a thing for blondes.

"I can't believe I'm doing this," said Annie, taking a deep breath. "Never in a trillion years did I think I'd be having sex with my husband's posse."

"Well, we sure thought we'd be havin' sex with you," responded Jimmy John. "It was jus' a matter of time."

"Do I come across as that easy?"

"No, ma'am. But any woman will do it if the situation is right. Like making a movie."

"A porn movie," she corrected. "I've always been tempted to do one. Just to see what I look like having sex on camera. But Archie was always shy about it."

"I ain't shy," Big Dog assured her. "I'm on television every week."

"But selling used cars," said Annie. "Not fucking."

"Practically the same thing. Lotsa people think I've screwed 'em on car deals."

Annie inspected her proposed co-star, a husky specimen standing well over six feet and weighing in at nearly three hundred pounds. She was tall, but seemed dwarfed beside the big man. "Are you that hairy all over?" she asked.

"Yessum. Hairy as a dog. That's why they call me Big Dog. But don't you worry, I ain't got no fleas."

"Well, you will certainly look the part for our naughty fairy tale," she giggled. "This will be my first time at bestiality."

Pinkie had been scouting the huge living room for a good location to film. "How about over here?" he pointed to a corner with a couch and ornate curtains as the backdrop. "This could be inside the Beast's castle."

"I got a castle?" said Big Dog in amazement.

Pinkie ignored him. "Let's forego the costumes and cut straight to the action. Think of it as the parts Disney left out of the movie. Annie dear, would you and Bill mind taking your clothes off for this scene?"

"You're the director." She began unbuttoning her blouse. It was quickly apparent that she wasn't wearing a brassiere as two creamy mounds of flesh popped into view. Her nips were like ripe cranberries, standing out against light pink areolae.

"Holy shit, look at them beauties," said Big Dog.

"Bigger'n I thought they'd be," added Jimmy John.

"Turn this way for the camera, my dear." Pinkie had already begun videotaping. "Let me get a good shot of those mammaries."

"You like them?"

"I'd love to suck on them."

"But you're gay."

"Yes, but I've always had a nursing fetish. My mama weaned me too soon, I suspect."

"Hand Ruthie the camera and I'll let you suck on them all you want."

"Maybe later," he demurred. "Right now I want to see you engaged in intercourse with that big hairy animal. It's so kinky."

"Your wish is my command," she quipped. Giving her boobs a little jiggle for benefit of the camera – and the cameraman.

"Hoorah, at last I get to see Miss Annie naked," exclaimed the giant. Eyeing her exposed breasts.

"You're going to get to do more than that," she reminded him. "You better get undressed too."

"Look at them tits," drooled Jimmy John, admiring Annie's bared assets. The perfect 34-Bs seemed to defy gravity. "I can't wait t' suck on 'em too. You gonna let me, right?"

"You should be paying attention to these," said Ruthie, shucking her sweater to reveal two magnificent mounds tipped with wide pink areola.

"My pleasure, ma'am," he grinned. "Mind if I touch 'em."

"Think of it as an undressed rehearsal," the blonde said, moving within easy reach.

By now Annie had stepped out of her denim shorts, leaving her in black G-string panties that barely covering her pubes. "Do you like what you see?" she said to Big Dog, striking a very sexy pose.

"I'll say."

"May as well see the rest." She rolled the G-string down her legs to reveal a wiry strip of hair. The Brazilian wax left her labia exposed, a vertical slit flanked by fleshy lips.

"That's a mighty pretty pussy," the big man agreed. He was down to boxer shorts, his furry body on display.

"Thank you, Bill."

"Ruthie, we wanna see your'n too," said Jimmy John, tugging at her short shorts.

"Easy, little guy. Don't rip my panties. You're going to get a good look."

Pinkie had been videotaping this all. "Bill, take off your boxers so we can get a shot of your mighty weapon."

"Aw shucks, it ain't that big. But it'll get the job done."

True enough, Big Dog Blankenship sported a twinkie, small in proportion to his large physique. Nonetheless it was standing at attention, ready for action.

"Oooo," Annie pretended to admire it, acting for the camera. "I'm getting wet."

"No shit?"

"See for yourself," said Annie, leaning back on the couch and spreading her legs to provide the camera with an unobstructed view. Using two fingers, she delicately parted the lips to reveal a moist pink tunnel -- a view usually reserved for her gynecologist.

"Holy cow. Can I put my finger in there?"

"Go ahead. I'm all yours, Mr. Beast."

Pinkie zoomed in to record the incursion, Big Dog inserting his thick forefinger deep into the pink cavity. You could see the nub of her clitoris, swollen with excitement. It wasn't every day she allowed a man who was not her husband to do this.

Big Dog began to frig her with a steady rhythm, the camcorder capturing every stroke on its digital chip. It made a quiet *b-z-z-z-z* sound, offset by the *swish! swish!*

swish! of Big Dog's finger.

"Oh my," Annie murmured, starting to squirm. This was more stimulating than she'd expected. Was it simply because it was a strange man's finger inside her ... or because this was being captured on video for others to see?

"You like that, Miss Annie?"

"Um, yes," she gasped. "Go deeper. That's it."

Ruthie and Jimmy John had paused to observe. Ruthie was fascinated to see her girlfriend in an intimate situation with this big doofus. For the past week he and his pal had been watching them sunbath down by the lake. Now here he was finger-fucking her BFF as if there was no tomorrow. She wondered how Annie's husband would react if he ever saw this video? Not good, she was sure.

"Okay, cut," shouted Pinkie. You would think he was channeling Martin Scorcese. "Let's move to the *événement principal.*"

"Huh?" Big Dog sat back, removing his finger from Annie's snatch.

"The main event," Ruthie translated.

Annie had trouble regaining her bearings. "Wait," she gasped. "Why are you stopping?"

Ruthie answered, "Because Pinkie wants to get some shots of you two actually fucking."

"Okay. But hurry up."

"Oh boy," nodded Big Dog. "I'm really gonna get to fuck you, Miss Annie? No pretend?"

"Yes, but you can't tell my husband," she cautioned. Sometimes you had to repeat things to get through to the big dope. Amazing that he owned an automobile empire.

Big Dog looked puzzled. "Ain't he gonna see our video?"

"No way. He thought we were kidding about making a porn movie."

"Too bad he didn't want to join in," sighed Ruthie. She still had a thing for Annie's hubby. The only way she'd ever get to sample Archie Andrews would be under the guise of something like this.

"Do you think we've gotten carried away with this porn video?" Annie asked. On the verge of getting cold feet. "Should we stop?"

"Don't stop now, my dear," cried Pinkie. "We want to see this Beast violate Beauty's perfect body."

"Well, okay. I'm curious how it will look on the TV screen. That porn star Tori Black makes it look so sexy."

"You look kinda like Tori Black," mused Jimmy John, a *habité* of the video booths at Ernie's Erotic Emporium back in Charlotte.

"Really? I think she's beautiful."

"Your pussy's mighty beau-ti-ful," observed Big Dog. "Can I put my weenie in it now?"

"Well, uh --" she hesitated.

"You've gone too far to turn back," advised her friend Ruthie. "It's not fair to get these boys all worked up, then stop short."

Annie smiled weakly. "I guess you're right. In for a dime, in for a dollar."

"That's my girl," winked Ruthie. Knowing if she leaked this video to Annie's husband, he might be good for a revenge fuck. She'd like that.

"Do I need t' wear a rubber?" asked the giant.

"No," said Annie. "You can go bareback. I don't mind."

"Oh boy." Bill Blankenship was about to satisfy his

fantasies about boinking his friend Archie's wife. He'd lusted after her for years but never had the courage to make a play.

"Get on with it," urged Jimmy John, thinking this could be the beginning of some regular action on the side. He figured they'd be tapping these gals regularly before summer was over. His wife didn't mind that he kept girlfriends on the side, as long as he turned over his paycheck on a regular basis.

"Scene One, Take Two," announced Pinkie, focusing the camcorder on the tangle of naked bodies. This would make good blackmail material, he was thinking. With this video to hold over Annie's head, she'd have no choice but give him a generous raise come next performance review!

"What d'you want me t' do?" the giant naïvely asked for direction.

Pinkie told him to lie back on the couch. Big Dog complied, his miniscule erection pointing skyward. "That's it," nodded Pinkie. "Now straddle him, Annie dear. And when I say 'Action!' ease down on that erect organ."

Annie smiled prettily. "I'm ready for my close-up, Mr. DeMille."

"Action!" shouted Big Dog. Jumping the gun.

"Hey, I'm supposed to say that," complained Pinkie.

Without waiting for a second signal, Annie lowered herself onto the big man's stiffie. "*Oooo, that feels good,*" she murmured.

"Yessum, it sure does," grunted Big Dog. "My dream come true." With each thrust, the shaft of Big Dog's penis disappeared into Annie's body.

Given all the exertion, one might have thought this was an exercise video.

"Holy cow, Miss Annie, I'm about to cum," Big Dog announced. "Better let me pull out."

"Go ahead and cum inside me. I'm on the Pill."

"No wonder she didn't object t' him goin' bareback," observed Jimmy John, fascinated by the bizarre sight of his hirsute friend fucking Archie Andrew's pretty wife.

"Enough about them," nudged Ruthie. "Big Dog's shot his wad. Now it's our turn on camera."

"Enjoy it, big boy," she murmured. "This is the only time you'll ever get to fuck me. I'm not accustomed to cheating on my husband."

Ruthie snorted in the background. She knew about Annie's affair with a TV weatherman last Spring. But she was too fascinated with the image of her friend screwing the big used car salesman to contradict her words.

Big Dog wasn't deterred. She said this was a one-time event, but women always said stuff they didn't mean. She was fucking him now; that meant she'd put out again.

Meanwhile, Pinkie zoomed in for a close-up -- *B-z-z-z-*

The skinny little man didn't object as she pulled him down on top of her, guiding his curved dick inside her.

B-z-z-z-z. The Canon FV30 recorded it all.

≈≈≈

Everybody was stark naked, except for Pinkie. They were sitting there in the rec room watching their video handiwork for the third time when they heard the crunch of tires on the crushed-gravel driveway outside.

"Ohmygod, Archie's back," said Annie, grabbing her scraps of clothing and racing up the stairs.

"Better make yourself scarce, boys," Ruthie advised. "You don't want Archie to catch you with your peckers hanging out."

The two men scrambled toward their respective rooms.

Pinkie was busily tidying up the living room, spraying a whiff of Airwyck to hide the pungent smell of sex. Ruthie placed a throw pillow over the cum stains at one end of the couch. Stray underwear was stuffed into an ottoman.

They could hear Archie's footsteps on the front porch. Quickly, Ruthie paused the camcorder, disrupting its display on the TV screen.

Just in time.

"Honey, I'm home," Archie gave the old sit-com greeting as he stepped into the house.

"Hi, Archie. How was that man with a dog?" said Ruthie, standing there in her birthday suit.

"Dog was fine," he replied, eyeing the exposed alabaster skin. "Why're you naked? I didn't expect such a warm welcome."

"Oh, I'd give you a welcome you'd never forget, if only you'd cooperate."

"You'd probably wanna videotape it," he chided. A reference to their earlier joking about making a porn video.

"That would be fun. But I'm not even sure where to find my camcorder, I haven't used it in so long." She crossed her fingers behind her back. The pose served to accentuate her pink-tipped breasts.

"So what are you doing without any clothes on?" he returned to his original question.

At that moment Pinkie strolled out of the rec room, clad in his red Bermuda shorts and that T-shirt about the AIDs walkathon. The rumbled tee still had mustard stains on it from yesterday's cookout. "I was giving Ruthie a massage," he offered. "I'm very good at backrubs. Perhaps I should have been a physical therapist."

"Oh," Archie shrugged. "Where's Annie?"

"Here I am," she said, coming down the stairs in her black Lycra shorts and a fishnet top that revealed her breasts. The cranberry nips swayed like semaphore flags with each step down the carpeted stairs. "You're back early."

"Am I in time to watch any of *Hello, Dolly!*?"

"Too late, I'm afraid," said Pinkie. "You missed one of Miss Barbra Streisand's greatest performance. Even Jimmy John and Big Dog loved it."

That set off Archie's bullshit detector. No way those two rednecks liked a Barbra Streisand musical. It wasn't in their genes. "Where are them good ol' boys?" he asked, poking his head into the rec room.

"Oh, around," Ruthie said vaguely.

Archie noticed the PAUSE light blinking on the DVD player under the widescreen TV. "Thought you said you'd finished watching *Hello, Dolly!*," he said, picking up the remote control and pressing PLAY.

The screen came to life. There in 1480 pixels-per-inch living color was his wife, totally naked, sandwiched between his two redneck friends. Big Dog was sucking greedily on one of her breasts and Jimmy John was boinking her from behind. Prima facie evidence of their misdeeds.

"Looks like you made that X-rated video after all," he said, eyes unable to leave this scene of his wife performing like a porn star.

"I can explain," Annie said. But of course she couldn't.

"Annie, you screwed my two best friends?"

"It wasn't like that. We told you we were going to make an X-rated video. We thought you were cool with it."

"With my wife having sex with other men?"

"Dear, how else do you make an adult video? It was just for fun, something to do on this dreary old morning."

"You could've played Scrabble or Monopoly."

"We tried to get you to be in the video with us," Ruthie interjected.

"You stay out of this, Ruthie."

"Hard to do. I'm in the video with Annie and your two pals. Pinkie directed."

Archie turned to the little man. "I expected you t' have

145

better sense, Herman."

"It was just a lark," Herman "Pinkie" Roberts responded, his voice a slightly higher pitch than usual. "Perhaps we got carried away in our efforts for authenticity, but it wasn't mean to be anything serious, I assure you."

"Guess I'd better watch the whole thing," said Archie settling back on the couch, inches from the hidden cum stains. "You want to rewind it for me, Herman?" "Yes, indeed. I'd like to call your attention to the fine camera work --"

"Shut up, Herman."

"Do you want to watch it by yourself?" asked his wife. "We can go in the living room and give you privacy."

"No, everybody take a seat. We're going to have a World Premiere. Somebody go fetch Jimmy John an' Big Dog. Then Herman can roll the film displaying his great camera work on -- what's the name of this opus?"

"*Beauty and the Beast,*" squeaked Pinkie. "Clever, huh?"

"Let me guess who is who."

"It was meant to be a wicked fairy tale," Annie explained lamely. "With sex."

Ruthie came back into the rec room, leading the two shamefaced men. "Archie, let me explain --" began Jimmy John.

"Annie's already explained," he cut the man off. "Y'all was jus' makin' a porn video like you said you was gonna do."

"That's it exactly," Jimmy John nodded. Seizing this explanation like a lifeline.

"Big Dog, what d' you have t' say 'bout this?"

The big man ducked his head. "Jeez, Archie, you know I've always wanted to fuck Annie, she's so pretty an' all."

"Shut up, Big Dog," hissed his cousin. "That ain't the way t' tell it."

"But it's true. An' Annie said it was all right 'cause we was jus' funnin' around, making a porn video. I jumped at the chance, her sayin' I could fuck her this one time for the filum. Said it would be the only time I'd ever get t' do her, so I couldn't say no."

"Thanks for your honesty," Archie sighed.

"Ready to watch the video?" asked Pinkie, finger on the PLAY button. "It's about ten minutes long. Bill Blankenship is subject to premature ejaculation, so it didn't --"

"No need for the technical details," Annie's husband waved the words away. "Jus' play it."

9

Soggy Bottoms Blues

They had been shooting a fashion spread in the British Virgin Islands, a new line of eveningwear by Bobalino Cavetti. Today being a holiday, the crew decided to go over to a bar on one of the many islands that dotted the sea around Tortola.

The head of the ad agency – a white-haired old roué named Carson McCruthers – rented a motor skiff to ferry them across. There were six in all, Estella and another model, Carson and three of his agency cronies. The photo crew stayed behind, scouting new locations for the next day's shoot. The estate they had planned to use burned down the week before they got to BVI.

Bright yellow sunlight made it a beautiful day, dancing on the turquoise water like foxfire. Salt stung their skin as the skiff raced across the short distance to their destination. They were going to a beachside bar on an island that was jokingly called Dick Van Dyke because of all the romantic interludes that took place there. Likewise its popular inn was known as Chitty Chitty Bang Bang. Or in some versions, Clitty Clitty Bang Bang. Its official name was more mundane, Sam's Bed & Breakfast, although it hadn't served breakfast in twenty years.

Carson pulled the skiff into a half-moon bay, so shallow the water only came up to your chest. "Here we are," he announced. "The Soggy Bottom Bar." They could see the Tiki shack from here, a ramshackle construct of weathered boards and palm fronds that served every rum drink imaginable.

"How do we get there," his art director wanted to know. There was no pier or docking facilities in sight.

"That's why they call it the Soggy Bottom," Carson laughed. "You have to swim in. By the time you plant your bottom on a bar stool it's pretty soggy."

"We'd better put on our swimsuits," said the other model, a stunning blonde who went by the hyphenate name of Jean-Marie.

"Who needs 'em?" said Carson, peeling down to bare skin.

His companions were a bit taken aback, seeing their noble leader's dick on display. But his account rep said, "Oh well, why not?" and began to undress.

Not one for modesty, Estella was quick to follow suit.

The six of them jumped into the placid water, finding that it was shallow enough to wade, deep enough to stave off the embarrassment of being naked in front of your co-workers. Half swimming, half walking, they made their way to the sandy beach.

The Soggy Bottom had seen it all. The bartender – one Albert J. Foxworthy, better known to his patrons as Foxy – didn't bat an eyelash. Merely served up an assortment of rum punches with colorful names like Deadman's Delight and Knock You On Yer Ass Grog.

"To another three days of shooting – pray it doesn't rain," toasted Carson. A tropical storm was lurking to the south, too far away to affect the weather yet, but chugging in this direction at 12 MPH.

It was quite a sight, all those naked bodies sitting around the bar. Turns out, they were the only customers this morning. Boating traffic came in went in unpredictable patterns. Estella's was the only brown skin among the pasty white. The guys were studiously making an effort not to stare at her big glorious boobs. Or Jean-Marie's ample additions.

The art director bought a throwaway camera from a Kodak display behind the bar and said, "Let's memorialize today with a few pictures."

"Naked?" said the agency's fashion coordinator. More comfortable with haute couture than bare skin.

"Don't be a pill," said Carson. "We're here to let our hair down, right?"

"Yes, of course," she said quickly. Wanting to look like a team player to the boss.

"Go ahead," said the account exec. "Get a group shot."

Fl-s-s-k! – he got a great shot of everybody crowded around the bar, legs crossed for modesty, holding up tall glasses of rum in a cheery salute.

"Now get one of me with the models," said Carson. Wrapping a meaty arm around both girls. A dirty old man with his boobalicious entourage.

Fl-s-s-k!

"How about one of just me and Estella," he suggested. "Okay with you, hon."

"Why not?"

As Estella Szardoz smiled for the camera, the old lecher pressed his cheek next to hers and reached around to cup her breasts in both hands. Uh-oh.

Fl-s-s-k!

"There, that was great."

"How about one with me?" the account rep opted. Grabbing Estella's boobs like they were large bocce balls.

"Sure," she agreed. Serving up another smile. Unmindful of the familiarity of his hands.

Fl-s-s-k!

"Okay, take over the camera," the art director said, handing it to the fashion coordinator. "I want one with her too."

Another pair of hands found her boobs. Deep breath, smile, count to three.

Fl-s-s-k!

"Those are pretty risqué," commented the fashion coordinator. Proving that she was indeed a pill.

"Oh, we can do better," said Carson. Deliberately needling her. "Your turn Deidre."

"What – ?"

"C'mon, give the camera back to Burton and step over here for a company portrait."

The mousy brunette gritted her teeth as her boss fondled her apple-sized boobs for the camera. Breaking all company policies on sexual harassment, but being they were outside the US of A those rules obviously didn't apply.

Fl-s-s-k!

"You can't show that to anybody back at the office," Deidre squeaked.

"Loosen up," Carson laughed. Obviously having fun at

her expense. Speculation around the water cooler said that she was a certified lesbian, although no one had any proof. "Who wants to push the limits?"

"You want a naughty photo?" Estella volunteered. "I'll give you one you won't dare show your wife."

"Great! I admire courage," he said, eyeing the fashion coordinator pointedly.

Estella knelt down in front of Carson McCruthers and took hold of his cock. She was surprised to find it had the beginnings of stiffness about it, but that merely made her task easier. "How about this?" she said, placing her pink lips next to the purple glans as if about to perform fellatio on him.

Fl-s-s-k!

"Excellent, my dear. But why not go all the way?"

She looked up at their audience and shrugged as if to say, "What's a girl gonna do?" – then engorged the entire length of his phallus in her mouth. *Gulp!*

"Holy Jesus," said the art director as he took the picture.

Fl-s-s-k!

"She's really going down on him," sputtered the account exec.

"Oh my," wheezed the fashion coordinator.

"Anybody want another round?" asked the bartender as if oral sex among his clientele was commonplace.

"Yes," said Jean-Marie. "Another Killer Diller with a slice of lime, please." Trying to get in a little fortification before her turn at bat.

"Oh my," repeated the fashion coordinator. Realizing that she would be called on to participate too.

"Keep going, Estella." And to his art director: "Finish the roll on us, Burton. Get me cumming in her mouth. Then buy another camera to get some pix of Deidre and Jean-Marie with you guys. These will make great souvenirs of our outing."

Fl-s-s-k!

~ ~ ~

Couture Age ran one of the photographs in its "On And Off The Runway" section: A full-color photo of Estella Szardoz going down on the head of a large Madison Avenue advertising agency. A black bar covered his penis for delicacy's sake, but there was no question about what was going on here. No one knew exactly how the rag got hold of these incriminating picture, but fashion coordinator Deidre Brown was a strong suspect.

Roman Szardoz laid the clipping on the breakfast table in front of his wife. "My company's PR firm came across this."

Estella leaned forward to study the image. Nice color balance, good composition, quite sexy. All in all, an interesting picture except for that stupid black bar. "Yes, that's me," she confirmed. "And that's Carson McCruthers, CEO of Waumbach, McCruthers & Fitz. Picked as Adman of the Year by the FAAC."

"This is what you do on location shoots?"

"No, silly. Carson was just having fun with his finicky fashion coordinator. Trust me, there wasn't any serious sex going on."

He eyed her like he'd just encountered a visitor from

another planet. "How's giving a guy a blowjob not serious?"

"We were simply playing around. There was no romance, no lust, no nothing."

"Did he cum?"

"Well, yes. But that was inadvertent to putting Deidre Brown to the test."

"Inadvertent – ?"

"You suck on a willy long enough, it happens. I don't have to tell you that. But the intent was to back that lipstick lesbian into a corner, force her to have sex with a male. In this case, three males."

Szardoz put on his most patient expression, one that psychotherapists go to school for years to perfect. "And did she? Have sex with the men, that is."

Estella giggled. "Uh-huh. They all three nailed that little muff-diver. Had her moaning like a cat in heat."

"And you?"

"What about me?"

"Did they have you moaning like a cat in heat?"

She realized this was a trap, but she couldn't see a clear route of escape. "More purring like a kitten," she admitted.

"With all three guys?"

"No, of course not. I was only helping Carson out. Not participating in an orgy."

"Did anybody get fucked – you included?" he pressed the point.

"I told you Deidre got banged by all three men. And Jean-Marie did the art director."

"And you?"

"I just watched – "

" – after you blew the head of the ad agency."

"Dear, you make it sound like it was a bad thing."

10
Rubber Chicken And Condoms

"**C**ongratulation, girl!" said Cousin Donald. "You jus' got accorded a most singular honor."

"For what?" replied Gracie. "Did I win the Publishers Clearing House Sweepstakes?" She'd been reading a romance paperback while sunning topless in the backyard. The thick pine trees that flanked the house offered all the privacy in the world. Nobody around but Cousin Donald. And she didn't care if her husband's not-quite-right-in-the-head cousin saw her boobs. He was harmless ... wasn't he?

"Don't start spending that ten million dollars too quick. I'm talking 'bout them boys down at the Moose Lodge. They done voted you The Girl They'd Most Like To Fuck."

"Cousin Donald – !"

"Don't yell at me. It's your pretty round butt that won the vote."

"I'm flattered," Gracie said. "But I think Dave might object to my holding that title."

"He voted too. Matter of fact, it was unanimous."

"Really?"

"Nobody else came close. Not even Betty Ann Bentley."

"That's because everybody has already fucked Betty Ann," she observed cattily.

"Maybe so, but there was a lotta discussion 'bout other local women folk an' you won hands-down. There was even talk of auctioning off your favors as a fundraiser."

"Pish. Dave would never go along with that."

"Don't be too sure. He's treasurer of the fundraising committee. And the Lodge's coffers are at an all-time low."

~ ~ ~

A few days later Gracie got a phone call from Graham Pinkney, a used car salesman who also served as grand pooh-bah at the Moose Lodge down in Bensonville. "Gracie honey, got a favor to ask," he began in his overly familiar way. Like he was trying to sell a '98 Buick that had only been driven on Sundays by a little old lady from Augusta. A little too slick for her taste.

"Hi, Graham, what can I do for you?"

"A favor for your husband actually."

Gracie sighed. Poured herself a glass of wine with one hand, balancing the phone with the other. "A favor for Dave? Why doesn't he ask me himself?"

"Well, I think he don't wanna influence your decision."

The Moose Lodge was the social center of the county. She considered its members a bunch of drunken hooligans who used the organization as an excuse to get away from their fat wives. But her husband was a member ... and *she* wasn't fat, was she?

"Quit beating around the bush," she told Graham Pinkney. "What's on your tiny little mind?"

"The Lodge's bank account is a little anemic these days. So we've decided to hold a fundraiser."

"No, you can't raffle me off," she said. Preparing to hang up.

"I admit we did consider that option – "

"It's not an option," she corrected him. "No matter what fantasies you horny boys might have around the bar while downing Buds."

"Calm down, honey. We decided to throw a rubber-chicken dinner. Charge $20 a head. Figure we can raise a couple thousand without sweating it."

"Where do I come in?" She took a sip of the red wine. A nice Yellowtail Shiraz.

"T'morrow night the fundraising committee's having a little backroom party. Something to relieve all the stress from planning that big dinner."

"So? Enjoy yourselves."

"That's the point, Gracie honey. We booked a stripper to entertain us, but she just canceled. Got held over at a club in Atlanta. We was wondering if maybe you'd fill in."

She hung upon him.

R-i-i-ng! R-i-i-ng! and *Ri -i-i-ng!*

Gracie ignored the insistent telephone while she poured herself a second glass of Yellowtail Shiraz. Hmm, delish. A full-bodied red wine all way from Australia.

Ri -i-i-ng! Ri -i-i-ng!

Je-sus! She answered the phone with, "Forget it, Graham. I'm not going to take off my clothes for my husband's cronies at the Moose Lodge."

"Girl, what the hell you talkin' about?" came her brother's voice.

"Oh. Hi, Bob. I was just kidding around."

"Didn't wanna talk t' you nohow. I was calling t' speak with your husband. He around?"

"Sorry, but Dave's down at Fat Fred's Lumberyard picking up some building materials. He and Cousin Donald are going to expand the storage room next to the barn."

"Tell him I'll call back t'night."

"Are you sure you don't you want to talk to me?"

"Maybe later. Bye now, Gracie Girl."

She listened to the humming of the telephone line after he hung up. Cheapskate, he didn't like running up long distance charges. But it wasn't like he had any other sisters than her. Ever since he'd got married, he had very little time for her.

Oh well.

She'd nearly finished off the bottle of Shiraz when the phone shrieked again.

Ri -i-i-ng! Ri -i-i-ng! Ri -i-i-ng!

"Look, Bob – " she began.

"It's me, Graham. We got cut off."

"No, we didn't. I hung up on you."

"C'mon, Gracie. Don't be that way. We're in a pinch here. We gotta find a replacement for that stripper. We done promised the fundraising committee that we'd provide entertainment."

"Forget it."

"C'mon, Gracie, everybody's heard-tell how you worked as a stripper to help pay your way through college."

"That was then, this is now."

"Don't be that way, honey."

"Get Betty Ann Bentley."

"I tried. She's visiting a cousin in Knoxville."

Gracie emptied the glass in one swig. "I'm second choice? Telling me that isn't the way to talk me into helping you out."

"You mean you'd consider it?"

The wine was having its effect. "Maybe. If Dave's okay with it."

"He said it was up to you."

Hm, she was still pissed with him for not taking her to Europe this year. She'd really wanted to spend a week or two in Paris. Maybe this would show him a thing or two about keeping here happy. "Tomorrow night?"

"That's right, at 9 p.m. In the backroom at the Moose Lodge."

"Will my husband be there?"

"Oh yes."

"Me too then."

~ ~ ~

"Sure 'preciate your stepping in at the last minute," said Graham Pinkney, a short man in a checkered sports coat. His mustache looked like an out-of-control fungus growth. His teeth had been capped, as white as tiny glaciers, and he smiled often. Getting his money's worth out of the expensive orthodontics.

"*De rien.*" Gracie liked to show off her University of Georgia degree in French Studies. She spoke the language with a perfect Parisian accent, having gone to school abroad during her junior year. She'd made good tips moonlighting at Atlanta's Sugar Baby Club.

"Huh?"

"I said it's nothing. Happy to help out."

Despite Graham's reassurance, she suspected her husband didn't know about this invitation to entertain the fundraising committee. He hadn't mentioned it at supper last night, so she'd kept silent on the subject. This unannounced ecdysiastical performance would probably embarrass him in front of his friends, but wasn't that why she'd agreed to do it?

For tonight's show she'd put together a special costume, one that ought to get everyone's attention. A G-string and tassels, just like a Bourbon Street stripper. Give these good ol' boys a few beers and they would be throwing dollar bills onto the stage at her feet.

"Fat Fred will let you know when it's time to go on," Graham was saying. "We got a few business items to tend to 'fore we get to the partying."

"No problem. I'll do my makeup."

"You look good jus' as you are."

"Sweet of you to say so, but I want to put a touch of gloss on my nipples."

"Lord Almighty! I can't wait to see that."

"Stay and watch me put it on if you like."

"Goodness knows I'd like to. But I gotta go call the meeting t' order." He looked like he could kick himself for turning down this – shall we say it? – titillating offer.

As Graham started to leave, Gracie put a hand on his arm. "I have a question," she said. "A matter of curiosity."

"Yeah?"

"Did you boys really vote me The Girl You'd Most Like To Fuck?"

"Uh, well – " His face flushed scarlet. "Maybe we joked around about something like that."

"And did someone actually propose raffling me off as a fundraiser?"

"It mighta been mentioned."

"Why don't you bring it up again tonight? After my performance."

"You mean you'll do it?"

"It's for a good cause, isn't it?"

"I don't think your husband's gonna like this."

She smiled sweetly. "Why not? He's the treasurer of the fundraising committee. I'd think he would support any proposition that might put money in the Lodge's near-empty account down at Wachovia."

~ ~ ~

Fat Fred Guzman stuck his head in the door and said, "You're on, li'l lady."

Gracie followed him down the hallway, the hem of her red gown brushing against the dusty floor. Peeking inside the dimly-lit backroom, she could see that a makeshift stage had been set up in a near corner. Half-a-dozen local men sat around the tables, chatting, upending sweaty bottles of Budweiser – the beer of choice at the local Moose Lodge.

She recognized them all: Elmer Parsons and Lawrence Absher, both small businessmen in Bensonville. A neighbor from North Bensonville, a chicken farmer named Tom

Carson. Graham Pinkney, of course. And then her husband sitting next to Cousin Donald. What was that demented loon doing here? She hadn't planned on stripping in front of her husband's retarded cousin. Donald was always trying to sneak peaks of her sunning topless in the backyard -- the pervert!

"Do they know I'm tonight's entertainment?" she whispered to her guide.

"No ma'am," grinned the big lumberman. "Graham thought he'd let it be a surprise. Ain't often we get a local gal to party with us."

"How about my husband?"

Fat Fred grinned. "He's gonna be most surprised of all."

Hm, just as she'd thought. Graham had been setting her up. A comeuppance for his pal Dave, getting his wife to take off her clothes in front of his Lodge brothers. Cute, but she'd certainly upped the ante by agreeing to be auctioned off.

Fat Fred must have been thinking the same thing. "Is it true you're going along with that auction idea?" he asked.

"Better get your checkbook out."

The wealthy lumberman smirked. "Oh, I think I can outbid these piss-poor shopkeepers and farmers. You may as well count on spending the night with me, li'l lady."

"Why, Fred Guzman, I didn't know you wanted to get in my panties."

"What guy in the county don't?"

She smiled, brushing against him. "You mean I might get to find out why they call you *Fat Fred*?"

"Ain't jus' the size of my bank account," he boasted.

No, it's the 300 pounds of blubber you carry around, she thought. But instead she said, "That big bank account's going to come in handy. My favors don't come cheap."

"Hell, I can afford it," he said, patting her on the rump. "I own half the land 'tween here and Macon."

"Let's see how the auction goes," she said sweetly. Trying to ignore the hand on her ass. "But first I have a dance to do."

"You gonna get plumb naked?"

"Maybe."

"That I surely wanna see," he chuckled. Giving her bottom a little squeeze.

"Here," she said, handing him a cassette titled *The Best of Patsy Cline*. A country music fan, her brother Bob had left it behind on his last visit to North Bensonville. "Put this on. I'll come out when I hear it start playing."

"Gimme a second. The tape player's on the other side of the room." He took the cassette and slipped into the semi-darkened room, a Goodyear blimp moving through the twilight.

At least the fat lumberman was no longer feeling her up. *Ugh!* – the things she did to get back at her husband.

"*Cra-zy* – " began the Patsy Cline song. A favorite of these Grand Ole Opry aficionados. Gracie stepped through the door and mounted the stage, a platform constructed from flat sheets of 3/4" plywood laid across concrete blocks. There was a smattering of comments like "Look-ee here!" and "It's time to party!" until they recognized her as Dave's wife.

"Damn my eyes," said Elmer Parsons, a local furniture dealer. A goofy grin spreading across his moon-pie face as Gracie took center stage. "Ain't that Gracie Harold?"

"You dog," said Lawrence Absher. A bugeyed man who owned the Benjamin Moore paint store in Bensonville. "This is your way of teasing us after voting your wife as our dream girl, ain't it?"

"Well – " Dave was at a loss for words. What'n hell was going on here?

"Gracie volunteered to pinch hit when our stripper canceled," explained Graham in a cautious tone. Not sure how Dave would take this unscheduled exhibitionism by his wife. "Said she wanted to show her support for our fundraising efforts."

"That ain't all she's gonna show," commented Fat Fred. Grinning like an oversized Buddha.

"Is she really gonna strip?" asked Lawrence. Eyes as shiny as new quarters.

"Yep," said Graham effusively. "That's the deal."

"Completely naked?"

"Dunno. That's up to her."

"Goddamn, a member's wife taking her clothes off for us," crowed Tom Carson. "That's a first."

"Dave, this is mighty generous of you," said the furniture dealer. "A striptease is just the thing to relieve a little stress at the end of a hard week."

"Just the thing indeed," agreed the paint-store owner. Lawrence playing Tweedledum to Elmer's Tweedledee.

"But – " Dave began.

"*Shhhh,*" said Cousin Donald. "Let's see how far the girl's willing t' go."

"I'm afraid to find out," Dave Harold muttered, so quiet he could have been talking to himself.

The music continued: "*I'm cra-zy – *" Ol' Patsy crooning out a world of heartbreak and sadness. Up on the stage Gracie was swaying in time to the music.

"C'mon, honey, show your stuff," called Graham.

"Take it off," shouted Fat Fred.

Obligingly, she unbuttoned her red gown down the front. Exposing an unbroken stretch of skin that indicated she wasn't wearing a bra.

"Look-ee that, she's wiggling outta that slinky red dress like a snake sheddin' its skin."

"Hot damn!"

With an undulating motion Gracie slid the dress off her shoulders and let it drift to the dusty plywood floor. Leaving her in a tiny red G-string and pasties with tassels. Her breasts were full and round, the tassels swaying as she moved in time to the music. Fashioned from a window sash, she'd delicately attached the adornments with double-stick tape.

"Cra-zy for loving you –"

"God in Heaven," said Lawrence at the sight of her unfettered breasts. "Your wife's sure built, Dave."

"Thanks, I guess."

"Yeah, great tits," agreed Elmer. Mesmerized by the movement of the red tassels.

By now Gracie had sashayed over to the edge of the stage, almost within reach. Bending forward, she dangled the tassels in Elmer's upturned face.

He tried to nip at them with his teeth. "Uh-uh," she waggled a forbidding finger. Causing the tassels to sway back and forth even more. "No biting."

Elmer continued gnashing at them despite her warning. "Goddamn, those tits are big as cantaloupes," he observed from inches away. "Shake 'em for us, Gracie darling."

Stepping back, she complied with a motion that caused the tassels to twirl in a clockwise manner. She hadn't mastered the art of making them go in different directions at the same time, even though she'd practiced all afternoon in front of her mirror. But the audience seemed quite happy with her rudimentary twirling skills.

"Gee, Dave, you're a real sport. Letting your wife show her tits like this," gushed Lawrence. Not very politic, always running off at the mouth. *Ready-fire-aim*, his friends described him.

"Yeah, well – "

"How'd you talk her into it? My wife won't even undress in front of me, much less all my friends."

"You're forgetting Gracie's been a professional stripper," interjected Graham Pinkney. Not wanting to explore the topic of exactly who was responsible for talking Dave's wife into this mischief. "She's used to being naked. Ain't that right, Dave?"

"She done a li'l stripping during college," he allowed. Unsure how to handle this awkward state of affairs. Elmer was biting at those tassels again. Lawrence's tongue was hanging out like a hungry dog's. And Fat Fred was begging her to "take it off, take it *all* off."

"This is surely one for the books," commented Cousin Donald. Being a Moose Lodge regular, Dave's cousin served as a *de facto* member of the fundraising committee. "Wonder how far the girl's gonna take this?"

"Too far," Dave muttered. But no one was listening.

The tape clicked onto the next Patsy Cline track, a plaintive version of "Have You Ever Been Lonely (Have You Ever Been Blue)." Gracie began swaying dreamily to the music, a gesture that made her tassels swing back-and-forth like twin metronomes.

Elmer couldn't take his eyes off her breasts. "Goddamn, I'd like to suck on them titties," he said, ignoring her husband's presence at the next table.

"Behave yourself," she scolded playfully. Giving him an extra jiggle.

"Hard to do with you practically naked," he responded.

"Did you say you're getting hard?" she teased. Dancing closer to inspect his telltale tumescence.

"Don't mind admitting it."

"I know I am," rejoined Fat Fred. Grabbing his crotch to make the point.

Tom Carson's eyes were bulging. "Holy moley," he muttered aloud, leaning close to the makeshift stage for a better view.

"Like what you see?" she called down to him.

"Gotta admit I never expected t' see *this* much of you, Gracie Harold." Being one of the their closest neighbors in North Bensonville, he occasionally bumped into Gracie at the 7-11, passed pleasantries with her, and like most of the local men lusted after her from afar.

"Really, Tom," she chided. "I've seen you gawking at me over the drink cooler. You've already imagined what I look like naked."

"Ain't the same as seein' you here in the flesh."

"Then take a good look," she said. Deliberately thrusting her pelvis toward him. The tiny red triangle of fabric stretching so tight across her *mons veneris* he could make out the crease of her sex.

"Heaven help me, that's a mighty pretty sight," observed Tom Carson. He hadn't seen a naked woman since his wife died in a bizarre chicken-plucking accident three years ago. He'd been pretty much a monk since them, not even going down to Dirty Nellie's to watch the girlie shows.

"Thank you, kind sir."

"How 'bout taking off them tassels?" suggested Elmer. Still focused on her boobs. "I wanna see your nips."

"Yeah, Gracie. You promised I could see that gloss," Graham reminded her with an undisguised leer.

"Okay, boys, you've talked me into it." She plucked off the tassels to expose her areolae. *Ouch!* and *Ouch!* "There, is that what you wanted?"

"Them's cute as button's," Elmer complimented her dark penny-sized nipples.

"Glad you like them," she called down to him. Cupping her breasts as if offering them to him.

"Get completely naked," urged Fat Fred. "That's what I wanna see."

"Yeah, take off your pants too," said Tom Carson. Eager to see the origin of that crease in her G-string.

"I don't know about that – "

"Ain't that the whole point of a striptease?" observed Cousin Donald. "To take it *all* off?"

She turned to her husband. "Dear?"

Dave shrugged. "You've gone this far."

"Here goes," she said. Flicking a clasp that caused the G-string to fall away, fluttering to the floor like a dropped handkerchief. Revealing a tuft of hair, the puffy lips of her sex.

"Oh Sweet Jesus, look-ee that."

"Man o' man. That's a great-looking pussy."

"Thank you, boys," she accepted the compliments.

"No offense, Gracie, but I bet you'd be one helluva fuck."

"Elmer!" she scolded. "I can't believe you're saying that in front of my husband."

"Aw, he knows how we feel," said the furniture salesman. "We've all talked 'bout which girls hereabouts we'd most like t' do."

"So I'm told."

"C'mon, we were jus' joking around," backpedaled Dave. "Wasn't a serious conversation."

Gracie stopped dancing – ignoring the music – and turned to face her husband's Lodge brothers: "Is it true you boys voted me The Girl You'd Most Like To Fuck?"

"Yessum, guess we did at that," admitted the paint dealer. "But we didn't mean no disrespect."

"Quite the contrary," she assured him. "I'm very flattered."

"Really?"

"Really truly."

Elmer looked sheepish. "Somebody – I think it was Cousin Donald – even suggested we oughta auction you off to raise money for the Lodge."

Cousin Donald? That dirty dog, trying to get her in trouble. She gave him an accusatory glance, but he refused to meet her eyes. The coward.

"Too bad you're married to our pal Dave," grunted Lawrence. "Else we might've tried talking you into it."

"Oh, I might be more willing than you think," she replied.

"You serious?"

On cue, Graham Pinkney leaped onto the plywood stage. "Listen up, brothers," he shouted, sounding like a TV minister addressing his flock. "I've got a big announcement t' make. Gracie here has graciously agreed to go along with the auction. Just among us committee members. All proceeds going into the Lodge's fundraising kitty."

"What the fuck – ?" said Dave before he caught himself.

"Well now, ain't that a kick in the pants?" observed Cousin Donald. "That li'l girl's gone an' outdone herself this time."

Graham raised his hands to quieten them down. "You boys said you wanted to fuck Gracie Harold? Well, here's somebody's chance to do jus' that. But it's gonna cost you."

"She's actually gonna let one of us do her?" asked Lawrence Absher. Always the skeptic.

"That's what you'll be bidding on."

"You ain't jus' funning us, are you?" said Elmer Parsons. Finding this amazing turn of events a little hard to believe. Good fortune like this didn't often come his way. He was known as the Joe Btfsplk of Bensonville, a reference to that Li'l Abner character with perpetually bad luck.

Graham turned to the nude woman. "Gracie honey, d' you wanna answer that yourself?"

She stepped forward, oblivious to the fact that she was stark naked in front of a half-dozen of her husband's Lodge brothers. Somebody turned off the music so they could hear her better. "Gentlemen, I take your selecting me The Girl You'd Most Like To Fuck as a very special honor. But how could I possibly accept such an accolade without allowing at least one of you to fulfill that ambition? So I've agreed to be auctioned off to the highest bidder. To help out your building fund."

"Holy shit!"

"Damn, I'm getting out my wallet."

"Me too."

Graham held up his hands to silence the excited men. "Before we start the bidding I wanna offer thanks to Dave for being so willing to share his lovely wife with us. As our treasurer, he's gone well beyond the bounds of duty."

"Way t' go, Dave."

"Here, here!"

"You'll go down in history as the best damn treasurer we ever had."

Dave didn't look very happy, despite the compliments and backslapping. But he held his tongue, watching the scenario play out.

"One more thing," cautioned Graham. "Being that Gracie Harold's a married lady – and most of us have wives at home – we can't afford to let word of this leak out. W'all gotta uphold an oath of silence as members of the Loyal Order of Moose. What happens here t'night cannot be discussed with others. Not even other members. Is that agreed?"

"So moved."

"Seconded."

"Alright, the vote is carried – and therefore binding on all of you."

The paint-store owner turned to Dave: "You okay with this, pal?"

Dave shrugged noncommittally. "Up to her. She's the big philanthropist."

"It's all for a good cause," she mumbled somewhat petulantly. "Right, dear?"

Dave didn't answer. Simply glowered at her.

"Let's get to the goddamn bidding," urged Fat Fred. "I'm suddenly feeling mighty generous. I might wind up paying for that new wing on this building 'fore the night's over."

"We'll jus' see about that," said Lawrence.

"Yeah, let's get started," snarled Elmer.

Wasting no more time, Graham grasped Gracie's wrist and raised her hand into the air. Displaying the merchandise to potential buyers. "Do I hear an opening bid for this prime specimen of African womanhood?"

Hm, thought Gracie. Was this how slaves felt on the auction block?

"$50," said Tom Carson.

"Jesus, Tom, you'd have to pay more'n that for a hooker," Graham reproached the parsimonious chicken farmer.

"How would I know? Ain't never paid for pussy before."

"Don't insult Dave's lovely wife. This ain't paying for pussy. It's a donation to the building fund."

"Okay, make it $100."

"$200," Elmer Parsons raised the bid.

"$300," offered Lawrence Absher.

"$350," shouted Cousin Donald.

"Hold on there, cuz," objected Dave. "You can't be bidding on a relative."

"Only by marriage."

"Still ain't right."

"Who says?"

"Me."

"Aw, it was just in fun."

"$400," Graham kept the bidding going. "Hope you don't mind, Dave. Like she said, it's all for a good cause."

"Yeah, right," muttered her husband. But he didn't sound very convinced.

"Screw this penny-ante stuff," said Fat Fred. "Let's cut to the chase. I'm willing t' pay $1,000 cash t' sample them sweet delights."

"Damn."

"Crap."

"May as well give it up, boys. I aim to have pudding for desert t'night."

"Well now, are there any more bids?" Graham called to his friends. Trying to keep the auction going.

"Dunno," grumbled Tom Carson. "That's a lot of money."

"Count me out," said the furniture dealer.

"Too rich for me," conceded the paint salesman. Business had been kind of slow. Not many fix-it-up projects this spring.

"How about you?" the auctioneer pointed to Cousin Donald.

"I'd best abstain."

Gracie surveyed what was left of the bidders. "How about you, Graham? Are you sure you don't want to put in another bid? I've seen the way you look at me."

"Got me there," he admitted with a blush. "Always thought you'd be one helluva lay."

"Satisfaction guaranteed," she promised. Ignoring her husband's scowl.

"Okay, I'm gonna go whole hog, raise the bid to $1,500," he said. Prepared to liquidate his 401K plan. "Anybody willing t' top that?"

"Come on, boys," said Gracie. Moving to center stage, still totally naked. Letting them see what they were bidding on. Ample breasts with chocolaty nips, flat stomach, long slender legs. Silky skin glistening under the yellow overhead lights. The cleft of her pussy on display for all the Lodge brothers to see. "Surely one of you is willing pay more than that to have bragging rights that you did little ol' me."

"I'm raising my bid to $2,000," announced Tom Carson. Stunning everybody in the room. Who would've thought this tight-fisted miser would put up that kind of money to screw Gracie Harold? Obviously he'd been lusting after his neighbor's wife.

"Tom, I'm flattered."

"Oh, I've got a tidy nest egg put away. Figured a romp in the hay with you might be more fun than a trip t' Myrtle Beach."

"You can count on it – if you win."

"Enough of this fooling around," interjected the lumberyard owner. "I'm upping my bid to $5,000 hard cash."

"Tom?"

"Shit, I'm out," said the chicken farmer.

"Beats me," admitted Graham.

"Anybody else?" Gracie queried the group desperately. Not happy with the outcome. "I'll throw in seconds."

That was it. Elmer and Lawrence had dropped out in the previous round. And Cousin Donald didn't count. But sex with Fat Fred Guzman – *yuck-o!* The man was 300 pounds of bloated whale blubber!

"Well, Gracie, looks like your pretty li'l ass belongs t' me," brayed the lumberman. Removing a foil packet from his wallet and slapping it onto the stage at her feet. "Got me a Trojan right here. You ready t' put it to good use?"

"Not so fast," drawled Dave. "I'll go $5,001."

"Hell you say. $10,000."

"Make it $10,001." Putting in a winning bid just as Gracie had known he would. She could always count on her husband to save her ass. Dave was nothing if not reliable.

"Christ, take it. But who'd pay that much t' fuck his own wife," grumbled Fat Fred. A frown shadowing his oversized face. "Ain't the American way."

"C'mon, Dave. Give somebody else a chance," complained Elmer Parsons.

"Yeah, why not let one of us sample the goods?" grumbled Lawrence Absher. "You already get it at home every night for free."

"Point was to raise money for the Moose Lodge," drawled Dave. "Jus' doing my part." Sounding as if he'd supported the idea of an auction from the very beginning. Yeah, right.

"Not a bad night," commented Graham Pinkney. "Ten grand will certainly help replenish our bank account."

"That's more'n we'll clear from that rubber-chicken dinner," somebody pointed out. "I think we all owe Gracie Harold a big hand of applause."

"Here, here," everyone clapped. Well, everyone except Dave.

"Thank you, boys," she replied as she daintily pulled on her red gown. "I'm glad you enjoyed it."

"How 'bout giving me a second chance," proposed Fat Fred. Not a good loser. "I'm still willing t' put up $10,000 t' fuck you, Gracie. That together your hubby's bid would give the Lodge more'n $20,000. A big number for the building fund."

"Well now, that's a mighty generous offer," noted Graham Pinkney. "We sure could use the money."

"I've got an even better idea," said Lawrence Absher. "Why not do us all? You lump all our highest bids together, that'd be better'n $24,000 all told." He was good with numbers.

"Holy smokes!" gushed Graham Pinkney. "That would put our finances on a Rock of Gibraltar footing."

"Yeah, Gracie," coaxed Elmer Parsons. "Do it for the good of the Lodge."

Cousin Donald was grinning wickedly. "Whattaya you say, Gracie? Jus' how generous are you feeling t'night?"

"Not *that* generous, you troublemaker. I'm not about to get gangbanged by the entire fundraising committee of the Bensonville Moose Lodge."

"Wait up!" said Lawrence Absher. Making one last attempt. "What if we pooled all the money and drew straws?"

"Yeah, how 'bout that?" pleaded Elmer Parsons. "That way at least *one* of us would get t' fuck you."

"Sorry, boys. Winner takes all. That's what we agreed. Dave, are you ready to take me home and collect?"

❄ ❄ ❄

ABOUT THE AUTHOR

Frank Holtzer has been called "an international adventurer" and "a lothorio of some note." Well, at least *he* makes those engrandized claims. As an experienced journalist, he's covered poverty in Port-au-Prince, Oktoberfest beer bashes in Munich, the swinging Carnaby Street scene in London, independence in the Bahamas, and the drug trade in Mexico. He's hiked across glaciers in Switzerland, whitewater rafted in Deliverance country, whalewatched in Hawaii, hunted submarines with the US Navy in the Gulf, cave explored in Appalachia, and treasure hunted in the Caymans. He swears that many of the risqué stories in this volume are true. You decide.

AbsolutelyAmazingEbooks.com
or AA-eBooks.com

www.ingramcontent.com/pod-product-compliance
Lightning Source LLC
Chambersburg PA
CBHW050401030726
47503CB00006B/1968